Teachers Abroad Mysteries

#1 Revolution Revenge
#2 Oasis Assassin
#3 Turkish Delight Gone Sour
#4 Singapore Fling

Singapore Fling

Phyllis Wachob

This book is dedicated to all those who love *The Maltese Falcon*.

Preface

Although some of the places in this novel are real, for example, the Haw Par Villa, Raffles Hotel, the Bras Basah Shopping Centre, most are fictional. The real places of Singapore are easily found in literature, in guide books or on the web. However, there is no Evernew Bookstore. In its essence, this is a work of fiction. Names, characters, places and incidents are either the product of the author's imagination or are used fictitiously, and any resemblance to actual persons, living or dead, businesses or establishments, events or locales is coincidental. Note: the Chinese character for gold is on the spine of the book.

Cast of Characters

Barbie Falcon: English teacher and amateur detective

Jon: her son, new college graduate

Georgia: Barbie's friend and former colleague, lives in Singapore

Matt: Georgia's boyfriend

Yannis: friend of Matt

Mr. Wu: calligraphy teacher

Bruce Lee: friend of Matt's and dealer in fake aphrodisiacs

Mrs. Lee: Matt's landlady

Xiao Yu: friend of Mr. Wu, owner of gold and antique store

The fat man: AKA the owner of the Evernew bookstore

Chapter One: Singapore Fling Goes Missing

"He's gone missing!" Georgia raked the red fringe out of her eyes with one hand, while wildly using the other to create a stir in the room.

Barbie stopped the toast from entering her mouth to quickly say, "Who? Who has gone missing?"

In answer Georgia took out her phone and shook it. "Matt. I've tried to get him for three days and there is no answer, no word, no phone call, no email, no message, no nothing. Nothing for three days. This is NOT like him. Therefore, I have concluded that he has gone missing."

"Matt? The…Singapore Fling? The current bf?" Barbie forgot about her toast and sipped her coffee. This crisis appeared to be heading towards a caffeine fueled encounter and she needed to clear away the jet lag cobwebs quickly.

"I'm going to check his apartment and I need you to come with me." Georgia sat across from Barbie at the table where breakfast crumbs and yesterday's mail competed for space. "I have his keys. He gave them to me just last week. I thought it was because our relationship was getting closer and that it was a step into more intimate encounters. But now I'm not sure that was what he meant. Why give me his keys, but then disappear?"

Barbie shook her head and the blonde curls bounced around her ears. She looked at Georgia and smiled. "Is that why you asked me here? To help you solve mysteries? Because, really, that's not what I do. I'm an English teacher. And right now, I'm on vacation, just visiting my friend in Singapore."

"Barbie Falcon, do not pull that, 'What can I do? I'm blonde and I'm cute and my parents named me Barbie?' stuff on me. I know better. Do not pretend to be an airhead. Help me here!" Georgia sighed.

"Okay. For a moment there I forgot who I was speaking to. You know me too well. Breakfast, shower and we go." Barbie took a monster bite of her toast and started to choke.

Georgia stood and half-heartedly slapped Barbie on the back, then ran to get some water. She glared down at her friend who was obviously trying to delay the trip to Matt's apartment.

"It's in Chinatown, so we can do sightseeing along the way," Georgia said brightly.

Fifteen minutes later Barbie emerged from the bedroom. She clutched her small day pack, digging for a tube of lipstick. She flung her arms wide, showing her three-quarter length khaki pants and a short sleeved blue tee shirt that matched the color of her eyes. "Is this okay? I don't know the customs here, but I figured that I needed to wear summer clothes and that showing a little flesh is okay? Not too much? After Turkey and especially Cairo, I feel that if I show two square inches of skin, I'm a harlot, and doomed to be sexually harassed for existing."

"Singapore is a modern place. We do normal here. Almost anything is appropriate, except at Raffles. Do you have your camera? Lots of interesting sights on the way."

As they walked the few short blocks through a maze of tall apartment buildings, Barbie noted the small shops. There were fruit stands, grocery stores, and kids' toy stores, stocked with as many books and educational toys as regular balls and dolls. They passed a small courtyard covered in tables and benches affixed to the cement surrounded by half a dozen food stalls selling a variety of cuisine. Georgia turned and slyly noticed Barbie's interest. "Yeah, you guessed it. Half the time that's where dinner comes from. Cheap, clean, nutritious and the government makes sure it is. It is almost as cheap as buying food and cooking in. You'll have many opportunities to eat there."

The sound of garlic sizzling in oil was joined by the smell. Barbie slowed as a Pavlovian response welled in her mouth and she felt saliva gathering and oozing from her lips. She licked them and then promised her tongue they would explore this culinary delight later. As Barbie tried to find the source of the delicious smell, she felt her arm rather rudely pulled and then a push propelled her forward. "Onward, onward," Georgia urged.

Barbie continued to walk, but soon fell behind as the landscape pulled her gaze. It was so different from any other place she had been. It was a city, but full of trees and grass. Covered walkways ran in all directions and pedestrians clogged the ones nearest the small shops. Some of the tall apartment buildings had shops on the ground floor and curiously, some had only sturdy load-bearing columns to hold up the massive structures. As they rounded a corner, Barbie saw one of these empty spaces being set up with chairs, tables and a dais. Huge pots were being settled onto portable gas burners at one end of the space, near the outside. "What is happening here?"

"Looks like a wedding. That space is a 'void deck', left expressly for communal activities. They have funerals too, graduation parties, engagement parties and just general hanging out. Interesting, huh? Very Singaporean. Come on, the MRT awaits. Here's a ticket." Georgia handed Barbie a thick plastic card embossed with a Hello Kitty theme in pink. "Don't lose it. Use it to go in and out. Automatically deducts the right fare. Here we go," Georgia said as they mounted a swiftly moving escalator down into the depths.

Barbie looked at what Georgia was wearing today. When they lived in Ankara, they all wore slacks and blouses and only when they were on vacation did they dare to wear something casual. And even then, it was jeans. But here in Singapore, jeans were too hot, too heavy and none of the other women her own middle age of 40-something, were wearing them. Georgia wore shorts, long red ones that skimmed the middle of her knees. They were loose and looked comfortable. But then, Georgia had a figure that made it possible to wear something like that. She was tall and lean, like an athlete, which she was. Georgia ran marathons. She also swam, she did yoga, she watched what she ate and she looked fabulous. Barbie realized that her longer khaki pants hid generous thighs and flabby muscles. No chunks of flabby flesh gathered at Georgia's knees, like they did at her own. No flapping upper arm wings peeked from under the cap sleeves on Georgia's short tight blouse. Barbie hid her own defects under a shirt with sleeves long enough to demurely cover the offending body parts. Although Barbie envied her friend's figure and athletic prowess, she did not envy her friend's attachments to the wrong men. I wonder if this Singapore Fling, this Matt of Georgia's, is another man of dubious talents and commitment?

The MRT train ride to Chinatown was short and swift. They barely had time to snag a seat when they had to abandon it as they approached the station. Georgia led Barbie confidently through the gleaming well-lit white-tiled station that had a half a dozen exits and up the most crowded escalator. A bright glare greeted them as they were thrown off at the end of a walkway with an overhead, plexiglas awning that protected pedestrians from rain. As they walked down into one of the oldest parts of Singapore, one that had hardly changed since the founding of the nation state, Georgia swore under her breath. "I forgot about Chinese New Year. It's three weeks away, but it appears to have managed to throttle Chinatown already. Look at all the booths going up. And the chaos!"

Barbie stopped at the bottom of the walkway and squinted into the sunlight. Three-storied pastel colored buildings loomed on both sides, creating a chasm that was rapidly filling in. Covered walkways made the street even narrower and now, the carpenters of Singapore were constructing temporary booths that reached even further out into the street. Goods stacked in boxes, wooden beams, awnings, temporary work stations of whirring saws and workmen shouting Chinese curses and jokes mingled with tinny music filling the space, creating Georgia's 'chaos'. Barbie reached for her camera but felt her arm jerked. "It will be here later. Onwards to the bowels of Chinatown."

Georgia led the way, slipping through the tiniest opening, pushing past and jostling anyone in her way. Within one minute, Georgia had sped ahead of Barbie and then disappeared. As soon as she realized that her friend was no longer ahead of her, Barbie halted. Standing on her tiptoes, Barbie lifted her head and swiveled it around. Tall and red-headed, Georgia was normally easy to find in a crowd, especially one that was short and dark-haired. As she turned around to face the way she had come, Georgia appeared from a side street that Barbie had completely missed, waving. "This way," she mouthed.

The alley that Georgia had taken was much narrower than the main street. It was wide enough for a car to drive down, if it weren't for the large trash receptacles, chairs, planters with shrubs and trees, umbrellas and a locked bicycle. A shallow cement drainage channel ran down the middle, periodically revealing a series of large covered drains, all of which gave off malodorous fumes. The two scurried along, avoiding the drains and trash, until Georgia once again made a swift right hand turn down an even narrower alley. This alley, too, was crowded with personal belongings, most set just beside the back doors that lined the narrow street. Georgia stopped halfway down and then muttered as she counted, "One, two, three, four, five. This one." She dug in her bag, produced a cheap key ring with two keys, mounted the two steps and inserted a blue key in the door. A tug opened the door outwards. She motioned Barbie inside as she pulled the door closed behind her.

Just before they were enveloped in darkness, Georgia slammed her fist against the wall, turning on the timed light.

The dim bulb helped them negotiate the narrow stairs that wound around themselves up into the heights. Barbie tried to keep track of the landings and how far they had come, when she bumped into Georgia. Her friend had stopped at a tiny landing where there were two doors, neither of which had any numbers or names. With a red key, Georgia easily opened the right-hand door. Barbie peeked over her shoulder as they took in the sight of Matt's apartment.

Light came from a large window directly in front of them. Shades were pulled to obscure the view, but not the light. A small couch sat directly under the window, its pillows on the floor. A floor to ceiling bookcase with built in desk was to the left of the couch. Every shelf contained something, a stack of books, mounds of paper, a dirty bowl and spoon, pictures, mementos of travel. To the left of the door was a tiny kitchenette with an apartment-sized fridge, an electric hot plate, a tiny sink, two cupboards and a used coffee cup on the countertop. Between the kitchen and bookcase an opening led to another room.

The air was hot and musty, causing Barbie to gasp. "Matt," called Georgia heading towards the other room. Through the doorway, Barbie saw clothes on the floor and sighed. Then she began to feel faint. Her heart raced, mist swept in front of her eyes, sweat beaded on her upper lip and under her clothes. Visions swirled in her brain that struggled to function in the close atmosphere. Visions from her past: a small boy's body in the alley, a cheap knife sticking out of his back; a pile of wet clothes floating in the icy water towards her; a twisted body lying in a ditch, blood pooling under the face. She felt an oppressive weight and she knew that in this place there was another dead body. She struggled to speak, managing only a croak as she sank to a heap on the floor.

Georgia's face loomed above her and Barbie spoke softly, "No, don't go there. Don't look! No, don't..."

Georgia cocked her head. "Matt's not here, he's gone missing."

Chapter Two: A Search of the Rooms in Chinatown

"Don't touch anything," Barbie whispered, trying to rise from her inelegant collapse on the floor. "We need to call the police."

"Absolutely not," Georgia countered. "No police. They are the last characters to be involved in this. Matt isn't exactly the 'lawful' type. Not that he is a bad guy, just that he operates on the fringes of the law, and society. Anyway, it's my boyfriend who took off. Besides, is there a crime here? A pool of blood? Weapons, drugs, a body? No, it's Barbie with a wild imagination. And overheated. I'll turn on the air conditioner." She headed for the bedroom.

"Don't touch anything!" Barbie called out.

"Okay, using my shirt to cover my fingerprints."

The sound of grunting and growling preceded a sedate wheeze and then Barbie felt a breeze waft over her. Barbie fumbled in her bag and found her water bottle. A draft of cooling liquid also helped clear her head. Georgia had switched on a small fan in the main room and within minutes the atmosphere became bearable.

"I mean it," Barbie reiterated. "Don't touch anything. Even if you can't find Matt, there may be clues as to where he went, and all your stumbling, not to mention my stumbling, may obscure something important. Now, is anything missing?"

Georgia looked around carefully. She pointed to the open flap on the built-in desk. A small drawer hung open, revealing its emptiness. "His passport and ID are gone, along with his wallet. His bag, it was always hung here," she indicated a small wooden protrusion over the desk. "His computer. He never went out without these things. His bag was big enough for the computer, it was one of those really small ones and there was a hidden pocket for his passport."

"What about his clothes? Is there a suitcase or backpack that he would have taken? I mean, did he plan to leave, and would you know that by what was missing?" Barbie asked.

Georgia tiptoed into the bedroom. "Suitcase and little sports bag are there, lots of clothes, not that I know all of his clothes. He usually wore pretty much the same thing day after day, you know, the ubiquitous jeans and tee shirt," she said as she came back into the living room. "I didn't expect him to go naked, wherever he went. I guess I just wanted to make sure that he was okay and that…"

"Another question," Barbie said, sitting gingerly on the lone chair near the desk. "Has this place been disturbed, or is it always like this?"

Georgia shifted her stance and looked at Barbie, attempting to look offended at this slur against her 'Matt'. Barbie's gaze fell on the cushion from the couch that was halfway onto the floor. A stack of papers lay on the floor, the top ones askew, and a newspaper lay scattered on the end of the couch.

Georgia slowly reentered the bedroom and reappeared rapidly. "Can't tell. He was not Mr. Neat, but this is a bit messier than usual."

"Okay, one last try. I don't see his phone, but maybe it's here." Georgia punched a quick dial and both listened for a phone ring. Georgia paced the room and bedroom, shaking her head 'no' at every ring.

Barbie cocked her head in a listening posture. "Shh, don't you think it's noisy in here, or is this place always like this?" She scanned the room, looking for the source of the low noise she heard. Her eyes latched onto the window, which was open slightly at the top. She then noticed moisture on the blinds and the back of the couch, as if rain had come in. "Wait, when did it last rain?"

Georgia thought for a minute and then shrugged. "Last night, yesterday afternoon. It rains about once a day this time of year. It's the rainiest season, not that it makes much difference. There are four seasons here, they say. Hot and wet, hotter and wet, hotter and wetter and this one, hot and wetter. It's strange that the window is open, but I don't think it is going to tell us anything about when he was last here." She reached up to push the window closed, but after three mighty thrusts, fell back. "You will not mock me!" she shouted at the window. She grabbed the chair Barbie sat on, pulling the back up and tipping her friend out. She shoved the couch aside and stood on the chair, putting herself closer to the offending opening. She looked at the window edges and then slowly pulled a piece of paper out of the edge of the window. She tucked the paper into her pocket and slammed the window.

She jumped down from the chair and harrumphed. "Who did that?" she asked of no one.

Barbie stared at Georgia and asked for the paper. "What is it?"

Georgia pulled the folded strip from her pocket and gingerly opened the sheet of thin, light weight paper. The rain had caused the ink to smear, but Georgia recognized it and whispered, "Jin."

"What does it mean?" Barbie asked, peering at the Chinese character.

"He kept practicing this character, the last three weeks or so. Over and over, like it mesmerized him. He practiced all the different styles. Jin, jin, jin, jin. This is just cheap practice paper, so I guess he threw it away and then used it to hold the window open. But why do that? Why prop the window open?"

"And when? How long has it been open?" added Barbie. "What else is here that can tell us something? The coffee cup? The newspaper?"

Georgia bent to pick up the Straits Times that lay on the couch. She laughed, "Last week's. We bought it together a week ago. That's no help." She strode to the counter top and looked into the cup. "Old coffee, dried up, kind of yukky. Does that help?"

Barbie looked around as well. "Was he here since the last time you saw him, or spoke to him, that's the question. If he left, was it of his own free will? Was he in a hurry? What did he take with him? Was someone else here when he left? In other words, did he leave alone?"

Georgia picked up the cushion from the couch, replaced it and sat down. "Those are a lot of questions. I don't know. The last time I saw him was three nights ago. We had our calligraphy class, that's when he was doing the 'jin' over and over. And then we went out to the bar down the street, on South Bridge Road, on the corner. We had a beer, or rather I did. Matt doesn't drink. Then he put off coming here. Maybe he didn't want me to see something or whatever, but it was so close, I thought we'd come here, not go back to my place. It was our time, after our calligraphy class. Kind of a tradition, like. But I didn't think anything of it at the time. Just tired or not in the mood and so what? But now…"

"So that was the last time you saw him? But did you talk on the phone since then?" Barbie asked.

"No, and that worried me a little. During the day, I didn't want him to call, in case I was in class or in the teacher's prep room. So, we often spoke about 6 or 7, if we had no plans to meet. I mean, we spoke EVERY day, especially in the last month. Sometimes we would talk right before we went to sleep. Stop giggling, Barbie. I told you, we were not like that. We were friends, we were really interested in each other's ideas and thoughts on things. He came from such a different place and when he listened to the news or read an article, he interpreted it so differently. And when he didn't call, or answer my calls, I began to get ticked. Then a little worried. And now, very worried."

"How did you meet?" Barbie asked.

"In calligraphy class. I found out there is a calligraphy society here and that they offer classes. Their website and literature are all in Chinese. But I went along, and the first night, there he was. I thought it a bit strange that he was interested in Chinese calligraphy, given his status and ethnicity, but he spoke Chinese quite well and it is fun. Being the only two 'foreigners' in the class, we sat together, and he helped me. The teacher speaks English, everyone in Singapore does, but the class is conducted in Chinese. Which I don't speak, not yet."

"What is his 'status and ethnicity'? I thought his name was Matt, like an American or English 'Matt'?"

"Oh no, his name is Ahmet, he's a Uyghur, from western China. Ahmet sounds a little like Matt in English, so he said just call him 'Matt'. Uyghurs don't like the Chinese because they are marginalized and harassed. I'm not sure how he got here, but he has a Chinese passport…and maybe another country's one as well. He is a persecuted man, without a home, who operates on the fringes of the law. 'Don't ask questions and you will be told no lies'."

They looked at the room together, trying to find something that could tell them where Matt had gone, and when. Barbie wandered into the bedroom and looked at the unmade bed, clothes thrown on the floor, an open wardrobe with simple clothes hung on hooks and a single straight-back chair. A few pieces of calligraphy were hung on the wall. They were obviously good ones as each sheet of paper had a small red 'stamp' in the corner with a simple signature. Barbie noticed the character, the 'jin' that Georgia had found stuck in the window, in a line of other characters, presumably a poem or saying. She bent to look at the titles of a stack of books that sat near the bed, some in Arabic, some in Chinese and some in English. Georgia was right, a very interesting man: erudite, well-read and a polyglot. She heard a phone chirping in the other room.

"Barbie," Georgia called out, "your phone is buzzing."

"Oh damn, he can't be here already!" Barbie raced into the other room and lunged for the phone, lost as usual in the depths of her bag. "Yep," she said, as she read the text message. "His plane has just landed. So, we have an hour or two, don't we?"

"Oh no we don't. Half-hour, tops, and he'll be waiting for us at the gate. It'll take us that long to get there. We have to go."

"We haven't finished here, there are still clues that we haven't explored. Don't you want to find Matt? But, you are right, we have to go." Barbie grabbed her camera and shot off a series of photos of the rooms and their contents. "Okay, now we go."

The two women scurried to the MRT station and fortunately caught a train immediately. The transfer at Outram Park also went smoothly and soon they were on the train to Changi Airport. Being the middle of the day, the train was not full and they found a two-seat space at the end of the car.

Barbie bit her lips, twisted her shirt tails, raked her blonde curls away from her face, held her phone in her hands and glanced at it five times in one minute. Georgia looked at her friend and shook her head. "Barbie, what's the matter? Are you feeling okay? Are you nervous about something?"

Barbie sucked in air, then let it out in a noisy rush. "You know that Jon went to live with his dad when he was fourteen. He'd always lived with me and until he was ten, his dad was basically not in the picture. Our marriage was precipitated by a pregnancy, and the relationship was horrible and short. So, Jon and I just did our thing, and we were fine. When the father showed up later, how could I be so mean as to keep him away from his son? It was hard. He was MINE and then I had to share him. Just before he went to high school, he said he wanted to live with his dad. I tried to protest, I tried to point out what a loser his dad was, but he saw the man differently. It was the hardest thing I ever had to do, let my son go.

"But we kept in touch and I never forgot his birthday or anything. I was mad and so disappointed. So, I guess to punish him, I left. I took the opportunity to go abroad to teach. What better way to get good experience than to teach English as a Foreign Language in a foreign country? But I missed him."

"But there were vacations, and skype, and email and photos and all!"

"Yeah, there were, you are so right. And a boy needs his father, a man in his life. But I still feel so guilty. I wasn't there for him."

"But it was his choice. And lots of people have to live with divorce these days, he wasn't the only one. Hey, Barbie, don't feel guilty."

"It's hard, really hard. I encouraged him to join me here, so we could have some time together. He changed his plans to come now; that was so good of him. He is such a good son. I don't think I ever did that much for him. In fact, I know I didn't. I never changed my plans for him. I have been a truly selfish, unfeeling, unloving mother!" Tears gushed form Barbie's eyes and made a messy streak down her cheeks. She hid her face in her hands as the other passengers surreptitiously glanced at her.

Georgia found a tissue in her purse and passed it over to Barbie. She patted Barbie on her back. She rubbed the shoulder nearest to her. She intoned meaningless phrases in an attempt to quiet her friend. Finally, she barked, "Stop, Barbie. Quit being stupid. You are a good mother. Hasn't he been away at college for four years? So he wasn't living with you or your ex. He's been on his own. Time for you to let go, anyway. Just relax. Think of what a good time you'll have together."

"I'm nervous and I feel guilty. What if he doesn't recognize me? What if I don't recognize him?"

"You and he can't have changed that much since you last saw each other, can you? When was the last time you saw him?"

"That's just it. I haven't seen him since he left to live with his father. I haven't seen my son in eight years." Barbie renewed her wails.

Chapter Three: At the Airport

"Mom!" The tall young man, blond hair flying, rushed towards Barbie, his backpack bouncing on his back. His arms flew around her in an enveloping embrace that threatened to topple her.

Barbie's reply was a muffled cry aimed at middle of his chest. She struggled to disentangle herself and breathed deeply. "My baby boy!"

Jon threw his head back and a great joyous laugh emerged, "I'm always your baby boy!"

In reply, Barbie squeezed his arms to feel his flesh, touched his face with light fingers, and patted his chest. Tears ran down her face as she whispered, "So strong, so handsome, and not a baby anymore."

Barbie took a gentle poke at a week-old beard, scowled at the mass of blond curls that needed a cut, and wrinkled her nose at the odor of 'needs a shower.' She turned to Georgia to introduce her son and she noticed tears pushing out of her friend's eyes. She smiled at the maudlin reaction she and Jon had caused.

They quickly found their train and within minutes were on their way back to Georgia's apartment. As Barbie sat next to Georgia, she gently teased her friend about the tears, "Why should you cry? We haven't seen each other in years, but you don't even know him."

"Like weddings, I always cry at family reunions. You sure recognized him right away. For someone who hasn't seen him in eight years, that is," Georgia riposted.

"Well, he sent me his latest photo on Facebook two days ago. Just because we haven't physically been together for a long time doesn't mean we haven't 'seen' each other. Skype, Facebook. I'd know him anywhere." She smiled at Georgia. "There is one thing about a long-distance relationship, though. You can hide things easily. But in person, up close, so hard to keep secrets." She smiled towards Jon who was standing and taking in the sights, balancing his backpack on his feet. "Thanks so much for having us both for a few days. I know what it is to have people in your space, so we'll only be here for a while."

At Georgia's apartment, Barbie bustled around making more coffee and rounding up sandwich makings. She insisted that she could manage if Georgia told her where to find things. She watched Jon and Georgia getting acquainted as they sat at the kitchen table.

"So, what have you seen on your travels?" Georgia asked.

"Magnificent scenery, beautiful architecture in the ancient monuments, cultures I had only read about. Poverty, dirt, man's inhumanity to man and his environment. Kindness, interest in me and my country, struggle for a place in the world. Life. Oh, fried spiders, smoked rats and evilly spicy chile." Jon laughed.

"And what is next after traveling for a while?" Georgia pressed.

"Graduate school. These days it's hard to find any worthwhile job without qualifications. I have given it a great deal of thought. I've taken the opportunity to read a lot these last few months, thanks to the new Kindle Mom gave me. I needed the break to figure out what comes next."

"And…?" Georgia pushed him.

"Law school."

From her place at the counter, Barbie jerked her head up and dropped a knife on the floor. The clatter and under-her-breath curse caused Jon to look up.

"And when did this occur?" Barbie turned to Jon. "Isn't it a bit late now? What kind of law school lets in late students? Not a good one. And why would you waste your money on a crap law school?"

"Hey Mom. It's done. I've already applied. To good ones. Don't worry about it. And I have grandparents who are quite happy to help finance it all." Jon grinned at Barbie. "Moving on. Got it together."

Barbie snapped her mouth shut and went back to cutting tomatoes.

Georgia helped put out plates and condiments and seemed to be pushing them along in lunch, clearing plates as soon as they were empty. Barbie snatched hers back and put another piece of cheese on it. "Are you in a hurry, Georgia, where's the fire?"

In answer, Georgia turned to Jon, "Are you up for a little adventure?"

"After a shower and shave?" he replied. "And laundry?"

"Great, I'll help with the laundry while you shower. Barbie, need any help cleaning up lunch stuff?? Thanks so much, by the way, for helping with the lunch."

"Okay, Georgia," Barbie said as Jon wandered off to collect clothes for laundry and to shower. "What's the 'adventure' you are promising?"

"I feel antsy. I want to go back to Matt's place. We didn't really look around. You said it yourself, we need to look around more. I am not overly familiar with Matt's day-to-day routine. I have been there, but not that many times, and I don't know what he took with him, if anything, and what he left behind. And his life is there. Whatever this mystery is, the keys to it are there."

"One thing we can do while waiting for the young man to become presentable is to look at any evidence that is here, in your apartment. Photos? Papers? Clothes?" Barbie frowned. "Notes, I think it is time to take notes. One more thing, try phoning one last time?"

"Good thinking." Georgia grabbed her phone and punched a speed dial number. They both listened to a recording in Chinese, then in English, that said that the phone was no longer in service. "Well, that's that. At least now I know he has gone out of range, dumped his phone, or lost it, had it stolen, or whatever. Now I think of it, the possibilities are too numerous to count. At least I won't bother calling again." She looked at her phone as if the malfunctioning of Matt's phone was the fault of her own phone.

"Photos?" Barbie asked.

"Yeah, I had some printed last week, the same day he gave me his keys. They're here," she said, reaching for an envelope on a small shelf in the kitchen.

Barbie took the stack of photos and looked at them one by one. They had been taken in various locations in downtown Singapore. In the background, Barbie could see the giant Singapore Flyer ferris wheel and the Marina Sands with a flying 'ship' on the roof, joining the three buildings of the complex. Some of the photos were of Georgia or Matt, but two of them showed the couple together. Georgia leaned over and pointed to one, "This one was taken by Matt's friend, and this other one was done with a selfie stick."

The 'selfie stick' photo showed their faces together, grinning stupidly at the camera. It wasn't centered and Barbie couldn't get the feel of the couple. But the one taken by the friend was more instructive. The two stood side by side, their hands casually linked. Georgia stood at least three inches taller, and looked even thinner next to the stocky Matt. Her skin showed a translucent, milky shade that contrasted with Matt's sun-tanned complexion. Georgia wasn't smiling, although Matt was, with an impish grin. A thick mustache covered his upper lip and a light beard darkened his lower face. Thick straight black hair fell over his forehead, melding into bushy eyebrows that floated above two thin lines, Asian eyes that had squeezed almost shut because of the smile. His shirt was blue plaid, short-sleeved and cheap looking. He wore khaki pants with a thin leather belt. Neither of them had their feet showing, so Barbie couldn't tell about his shoes. "Shoes, what kind of shoes did he wear?"

Georgia peered over Barbie's shoulder, "Sandals or cheap sports shoes. He had at least one set of nice clothes, and a pair of leather shoes, but normally he went casual." Georgia looked at Barbie and cocked her head. "Why are you asking so many questions about clothes?"

"When we get back there, you can tell me what is missing, or what is there. That may tell us where he went." Barbie looked back at the photo and finished making notes, including a note 'holding hands.' Why she included this was not obvious to her, but she did it. She found a few more good photos of Matt and slipped these into her bag. "We're going to find this character. He can't run out on you like this, leaving you in the lurch," she said in a fake, gravelly voice.

"Ready," announced Jon as he stood in the doorway, now dressed for the tropics.

"Pink shorts?" Barbie laughed. "Where in the world did you get them?"

"Sorry, they were the only clean ones. I got them off a Frenchman who was heading north. No use for shorts in China in the winter, so I took them. Okay, okay," Jon protested as Barbie continued her giggling.

"Who in the world wears pink shorts?" Barbie laughed.

"French men, believe it or not. No one else in the youth hostel would take them. But I now understand everyone's reluctance. Do I really look that stupid in them?" Jon looked down at the bright pink cotton shorts that revealed a lot of pale leg and clung tightly around the covered parts. "Maybe we can stop somewhere and I can get a new pair?"

"Let's go, pink shorts and all," Georgia urged.

As they got to the street, Barbie began to walk towards the MRT station, but Georgia called out to her, "Let's take a taxi, my treat."

Georgia put up her hand and within a minute, they were in a clean, quiet taxi. Jon sat in the front seat, but kept looking over his shoulder at his mother. A series of moues and jerks of the head communicated to Barbie that the ditching of the pink shorts was paramount as the taxi driver's staring was unsettling to Jon. Barbie leaned forward and touched Jon's shoulder, "He just thinks you're cute. Everyone thinks you're cute. We'll go shopping as soon as we get there."

"I know just the place," Georgia assured them. She gave directions to the taxi driver to drop them at the Yue Hwa Center, which turned out to be a shopping center full of small stalls selling cheap Chinese made goods. Barbie let Georgia steer Jon to a suitable place to find men's casual clothes while she wandered through the center. Stall owners sat with bowls of soup or plates of noodles or rice as they chatted with neighboring stall keepers. Mountainous piles of sheets and towels sat between stalls featuring tightly packed racks of thin rayon shirts and matching wide-legged shorts for women. Pots and pans vied with electronic goods in suspiciously worn cardboard containers and food outlets threatened to confuse customers with a plethora of packaged cookies, cakes, peanuts, candies, and chips. Barbie stopped at one and began to finger the packages of sweet snacks, straining to read the labels to make her selection.

"Barbie, don't need food now," Georgia said, grabbing her arm and steering her towards the exit.

Jon smiled happily as he displayed his new shorts, khaki colored, wide in the leg and cheap looking. "Ten dollars," he said, "Exactly what I needed."

"This way," Georgia urged as they crossed the street and plunged into the heart of Chinatown proper.

They came to Matt's alleyway from the opposite direction than they had taken in the morning and Barbie felt confused. The buildings looked too much alike and the crowds made it impossible to see street signs or other identifying landmarks. Barbie did note and remember a particularly vile-smelling corner near a dying tree in a pot just at the entrance to Matt's alley. Still, she felt the need of a map to get her bearings should she ever come this way again.

Jon followed Georgia without question until they came to the alleyway door and then he balked. "What are we doing here?"

"Georgia's boyfriend's flat and he has gone missing. We are looking for clues hoping to find him," Barbie stated matter-of-factly.

"Mom! This isn't one of your jokes, is it? One of your adventures? Does this entail dead bodies?" Jon shot back.

Georgia intervened. "No, no dead bodies, just a mysterious disappearance. Maybe he got tired of me and took off," she laughed.

Barbie and Jon stared at Georgia, neither believing the laugh was genuine amusement, more stressed-out reaction.

"What's the story about this alley of an alley? This place is population density on steroids." Jon tilted his head back to search the towering walls for some explanation.

"This is the heart of Chinatown, one of the original red-light districts in Singapore. It wasn't like American Chinatowns where the Chinese lived. The Chinese lived everywhere in Singapore. These backdoors are the husband escape routes," Georgia informed them. "The brothels along the main street all had to have these doors leading to the alleys. As you can see, there is no direct entrance to the main part of the building," Georgia continued as she unlocked the outer door. "There are only stairs from the top floor," she said as she mounted the staircase. "The story is that while the madam tried to waylay any wives who came looking for their philandering husbands, the word could be carried upstairs where all the small bedrooms were, and the offending patron could escape quickly down these back stairs and into the alley."

As they came to the top of the stairs, Barbie remembered the other door on the top floor. Presumably this door led to the rest of the building, leaving only this small set of rooms as an afterthought. "Are there still brothels here?" Barbie asked. "Is this one of them?"

"Yes, brothels are still legal in Singapore, and like everything else, tightly controlled. I've heard that there are a few left right here in Chinatown. But most of them are in other areas of Singapore. And no, I don't think this place is a brothel. There's a shop in the front and some offices and storerooms. I think Matt was the only one who 'lived' in this building," Georgia continued as she climbed the stairs and unlocked the door.

Georgia cautiously pushed the door inward and the three stood in the doorway, looking at the unoccupied apartment. Nothing had been disturbed.

"It's still cool in here," Barbie said as she walked into the small space.

"Don't touch anything," Jon ordered in a loud voice.

"What's with this family?" Georgia sputtered. "Barbie said the same thing. We've touched, okay. Crime scene contaminated. By the way, where did you get the 'Don't touch anything' phrase?"

"Television. I watched way too many crime shows. And my Criminal Justice classes," Jon explained.

Barbie looked at Jon accusingly, "Criminal Justice classes? When was this? You never told me!"

"Sorry Mom, just a few, in between the biology, philosophy and language classes. I needed something light to offset the rigorous things, let the mind relax. And besides, you were the one who introduced me to mysteries, so you shouldn't be surprised. I actually toyed with the idea of the CIA, but…"

"I see the detective snoop idea runs in the family," Georgia said. "Having experienced first-hand the 'Detective Barbie' in Turkey, I do understand." Georgia looked appraisingly at Jon. "So not just a pretty face, huh? Okay, no more touching. Barbie, do you have your notebook? Let's get started."

Barbie took out her notebook and stood near the door where she had a view of the entire living room/kitchen. "Walk us through it, Georgia!"

Georgia heaved a sigh of frustration. "Where should I start?"

"Start at the left and work your way to the right," Jon offered.

Georgia approached the fold-down desk that was attached to the tall wall-to-wall bookcase. "I've already told you that his computer, passport and ID are gone, along with the small bag he always carried them in. It hung here," she touched the corner above the desk. She opened the small drawer immediately above the desk again and put her hand in. She rummaged and found a small stash of coins and a crumpled $2 bill. Scanning the bookcase, she touched the spines of several books, but did not disturb them. She reached for a bowl with a spoon sticking out of it and gingerly brought it down to eye level. "Nothing," she announced. "And it's clean." She returned it to the shelf.

Georgia continued around the room, methodically picking up papers and rifling through them. She checked the newspaper again, flipping the newspaper pages in growing frustration. "Kitchen," she announced as she turned her attention to the corner collection of cupboards, countertops, small fridge and hotplate.

"Anything in the fridge?" asked Barbie as she scribbled in her small notebook. "Milk open? Gone off? Anything like that?"

"No milk, two oranges, a box of cereal, a stick of butter, some bread… That's funny, these look like the things we bought together, maybe the last day I saw him, or a couple of days before that. I don't think anything has been added to the food stash. And one dirty coffee cup. Does that tell us anything?"

Jon piped up from his seat on the sofa, where he sat reading the week-old Straits Times. "It may tell us that he hasn't been here in the last few days, maybe since you heard from him last. Maybe. Can you figure out what he was wearing?"

Georgia sighed, "I already did that. I don't know what he was wearing because I don't know his clothes."

Barbie accompanied Georgia into the bedroom this time and they looked at the small collection of clothes. "Are his good clothes here, you mentioned that he could dress up?"

"Here's his good jacket and pants. And his leather shoes. There's a pair of sandals and one pair of old sports shoes. I don't really recognize them. I don't think I ever really looked at his clothes before," Georgia whined in frustration.

"Here's the shirt he was wearing in the photo," Barbie said, reaching for the blue plaid shirt she had recognized from the photo. "Euww, needs laundering." She hung it back up on a peg.

"Something casual and like the rest of his clothes, I guess. I know he must have been wearing something. Wait, he had a light sweatshirt thing he wore when it was cool. You don't need a jacket in Singapore, but sometimes it gets coolish. It's not here."

"Good," Barbie said. "Give me color, description, anything you remember about it."

They returned to the living room while Barbie wrote up the latest in her notes.

Jon sighed and asked, "Where are we in this investigation? Time for the cops?"

"No," said the women in unison.

"It's not a thing for the cops," Georgia explained wearily to Jon. "He's not here, not on his phone, missing, not a problem for…"

The jiggling door knob captured their attention. The scratching noise of a key being inserted and turning in the lock made Georgia suck in her breath as the door began to open.

"He's come back," Barbie whispered. But the whisper died away as the blade of a large kitchen knife appeared through the opening in the door. Barbie's strangled cry rang out as the door opened wider.

Chapter Four: "He no pay rent"

"Mrs. Lee," Georgia stepped forward to meet the woman at the door. "How are you today? Is there something I can help you with? Something you need?"

As soon as Georgia spoke, Mrs. Lee whipped the knife behind her back, hiding it as inexpertly as she had brandished it. "I hear something," she said, "so I carry knife." Mrs. Lee was a woman in her sixties, with graying and thinning hair, her face lined with years of living hard. She wore the ubiquitous costume of a Singaporean woman of her age and class, a two-piece polyester blouse and baggy wide shorts that looked like a skirt. The pattern on her clothes consisted of small repetitive symbols, in subdued, colors. The two pieces did not match. "Where is he?"

"He's not here right now. May I help you with anything? Oh, these are friends." She turned to indicate Jon and Barbie. As she turned, she mouthed to Barbie, "Landlady."

"He no pay rent. Rent due. Now." Mrs. Lee stood serenely, as if right were on her side.

"Although he isn't here now, I'm sure he'll be back soon and you can ask him then." Georgia smiled brightly and retreated to stand near Jon and Barbie.

"Already two day late. He pay now," Mrs. Lee reiterated.

"I'm sure he didn't mean to be late with his rent and…"

"No pay, no apartment. I clean up, he get stuffs later," Mrs. Lee declared as she brandished a large plastic garbage bag from behind her back and began to lunge at papers on the floor, as if to sweep them up and dispose of them.

"Wait, wait," Georgia said with panic in her voice as she tried to intervene.

"You pay?" Mrs. Lee asked and waited. "Can or not?"

"Can," Georgia answered, her shoulders sagging with resignation. She turned and appealed to her friends. "What can I do? We can't just let her take everything." She turned back to Mrs. Lee, "How much?"

"Two hundred dollar, one week." Mrs. Lee smiled.

"Two hundred dollars a week," Georgia shouted, "for this place? There isn't even any hot water in the shower!"

"Okay, okay, one hundred fifty," Mrs. Lee smiled, showing two gold teeth in the front of her mouth.

Georgia reached for her purse and took out a wallet. She pulled out $20 bills one at a time and placed them in Mrs. Lee's outstretched palm. As she counted them out, Barbie watched Mrs. Lee's face. Tiny lines began to etch themselves on the corners of her mouth, happy lines of contentment, or was it greed? As Georgia handed over a final $50 bill, Barbie sensed triumph in Mrs. Lee's face and figured Georgia had been tricked into paying more than Matt ever did.

"And he will pay on time when he gets back, don't worry," Georgia added without conviction.

Mrs. Lee murmured a 'thanks' and shoved the bills into a front pocket. "And you close AC. Too cold already. And don't forget close lights. Electricity too much."

"Yes, Mrs. Lee, we won't forget. Don't worry. And, before you go, can you tell me about his friends? Mr. Wu, the calligraphy teacher, from the Calligraphy Society? Has he been here?"

"No Mr. Wu. I not know him," came the answer in a sullen voice.

"Well, you know me? I come here sometimes, I've met you. Here, talking to Matt. Did you meet other friends? Maybe a Greek man, about this tall," she asked, indicating with her hand an inch or two taller than herself. "His name is Yannis." She leaned forward and conspiratorially said, "Very handsome. Have you met him?"

Mrs. Lee jutted out her lower lip, "No, I not know him, I not know anybodies."

"That's okay. Just wondering. You have a nice day, Mrs. Lee. You take care now," Georgia murmured as she 'shooed' the woman out the door.

Georgia slumped against the door once it was closed and locked. "What a nuisance. What a character. I have no idea what Matt's rent is, but I think I've been had. It's tiny, it's a dump, it only has cold water, one AC unit. Really, $200 a week for this." She threw her arm in an arc to encompass the shabby rooms.

"That knife," Barbie said. "Did she really intend to use it on someone?"

"Tsk, she's harmless," murmured Georgia. "But she grew up in Chinatown, so I guess she feels she must defend herself at all times. Remember, this didn't use to be a very nice place. I'm not so sure she is a 'Mrs.,' but it's polite to give her the honorific."

"Friends?" Barbie asked then. "You are asking her about Matt's friends?"

"I just thought she might know something. If she had seen them, maybe she could tell us." Georgia stood pondering something, then turned to Barbie and Jon. "You remember I once said that I was attracted to 'bad' men, 'inappropriate' men. Well, Matt was one of them and his Greek friend Yannis was another. Matt is fascinating, but perhaps not always in a good way. Oh, who am I fooling? Trouble. He's trouble. But I kept coming around, and nothing bad happened, not really bad. Well, not so bad." Georgia sighed and crossed the room to sit on the sofa. "I should have paid attention to the warning bells; for example, I never did figure out where he got his money."

"He didn't have a job, you mean?" asked Jon. "That's not always a bad thing. I don't have a job. But I work and I earn money."

"That's the thing, he had money, he did things, but I'm not so sure you could call the things he did 'work'. And I don't know if the money he spent was 'earned' in the same way you and I think of earning money. He wasn't dishonest, he had a good soul, but there were incidents, friends, times that I had no idea where he was or what he was doing." Georgia sighed again. "I guess now that I am worried about him, I need to go back and think some more. This disappearance of his could be serious, or it could be 'I need to get out of Dodge for a while' or it could be immigration looking for him and he needs to disappear. I don't know."

"What does your gut say?" Barbie asked gently.

"My gut says this is different, this is serious. That's what I feel." Georgia started a low moan of frustration and anxiety. "He was working on something, I could tell. He was more secretive than usual the last few weeks. That's what was so surprising about the keys to the apartment. He was becoming a little more distant, and so I thought he wanted to cool the relationship a bit. But then he came out all lovey-dovey one day and gave me his keys. Now I think it was not because he wanted a closer relationship, but that maybe I needed to be able to get in here in case something…happened."

"What sort of thing was he working on," Barbie asked. "getting a job, helping a friend, what?"

"He would ramble on at times, telling me about the history of China, especially where he came from, Xinjiang. He would say that imperialists, Westerners, and in his case, Chinese, thought that history began when they entered a place. But of course, history is always, everywhere. He went on and on, telling me about kings and princes, warlords and invaders, poets and writers. And at one point, Uyghurs were known for being scribes and accountants, well-educated and sophisticated, traveling widely and trading everywhere. Of course, now they are seen as unsophisticated country bumpkins, but there was a time… And he would tease me with stories, telling only half and leaving the rest up in the air. I told him he was a Scheherazade and I wasn't sure I wanted to spend a Thousand and One Nights with him and his stories."

"But you kept coming back?" Jon inquired.

"They were good stories."

"Georgia," Barbie began, "what was his latest story, the last thing he told you?"

Georgia threw back her head and gave a howl of laughter. "The best one ever. Thirty kilos of gold."

"Surely he meant 30 pieces of gold?" Barbie said.

"The reference is to silver," Jon put in, "and it refers to betrayal. A well-known story and reference. But if he was a Muslim… He was, wasn't he?"

"Yes, so I don't know that he would have recognized the reference. But he had read Shakespeare, or at least studied it. I said something once about a 'pound of flesh' and he nodded sagely and said, 'Yes, our Jewish friend Shylock.' So, I know he was quite sophisticated and well-read in that way. But I don't know if he knew what the reference to '30 pieces of silver' meant." Georgia sat lost in thought.

"Was there anything else he talked about in the last few days you were with him? And, do you think these things are important?" Barbie pressed her. "This is a true puzzle. What kinds of things did he say or do that are important? And how do we know they are important? Only you can tell us these things. We've never met him."

"Well, I told you about the stories, and the secrecy, and then there are his friends. That's why I asked Mrs. Lee if she had seen any of them. She lives just around the corner across the alleyway, and I think she watches from her window. I think she knows more than she revealed to me just now. I KNOW she knows Matt's friends. She knows me; I've met her more than once. So, if Matt's friends have been here recently, she might know." Georgia gnawed at a hangnail. "Then there are the drugs."

"No, no, no!" Barbie said, alarmed at the mention of such things.

"Not in Singapore," Jon put in, "that's a hanging offense. Everyone knows that. Fatal, drugs are."

"Not those kinds of drugs, not heroin or cocaine or those really nasty things. I think they are more like aphrodisiacs, fake Viagra. You know, the Chinese medicine type of Viagra. They are illegal, but tolerated to an extent. He took me once to Geylang, the current red-light district, to deliver something to a friend, or was it to pick up something? I can't remember. Anyway, that's when I first met his Greek friend Yannis. Wooooh, what an experience. I was propositioned about five times in as many minutes. I think it's the red hair, green eyes, and white milky skin that got to them. It's illegal to solicit in Singapore, so the street girls can't say anything, they just walk around. And maybe because I was with someone who was Asian, they thought he was my pimp or something. If I ever get tired of teaching..."

"No, Georgia, you don't have to do that, ever." Barbie declared.

"Fake Viagra? What kind of a scam is that?" Jon quizzed Georgia. "Doesn't sound particularly dangerous to me. Was it run by the Mafia, or the triads or the local mob? That's what may make it dangerous. It violated their territorial space, or stole away their customers."

"Wow, I don't know about that. I can't believe that Matt was involved with the mob, but anything is possible. It didn't seem 'dangerous' when I was there, just uncomfortable. But I did not like his friends, that I can say. Yannis was okay, but the others left a bad taste in my mouth. Friends should be good people, not nasty..."

"How do we find these friends, nasty or not? They may know something about all of this," Barbie asked. "That's one of the first places a detective looks when they are skip-tracing."

"Skip-tracing?" Jon asked. "What do you know about skip-tracing?"

"I'll tell you later." Barbie turned to Georgia. "So, these friends, we need to find them."

"I'm not sure. I don't have phone numbers unless… Wait, Oh My God. How could I have forgotten?? Dumb, dumb Georgia. His other phone number! He gave me another phone number, months ago. I thought it was weird, two phones? But he only ever had the one, so I forgot. Maybe it's a friend's number. He told me that if I couldn't reach him on his regular phone, I could use this number. Where is that number?" Georgia rummaged in her bag and pulled out a small address book. She rifled through it until she found the page. "Eureka! Here goes."

"Wait, put it on speaker so we can all listen," Jon suggested. "And if you are scared or it's not someone you know, I can talk, you know, the big macho man. That is, if you want."

"Thanks, I'll keep that in mind. So, four, oh, six…" Georgia read the number out and dialed.

The three heads crowded together as Georgia finished punching in the number and pressed the call button. The ring could be heard in the phone. But also, a bizarre echo came from the opposite corner of the room. Jon turned and looked at the couch. Barbie followed him and then she, too, heard it. The unmistakable ring of an old-fashioned mobile phone.

Jon reached out and grabbed one cushion, throwing it to the floor, then the other. The noise became louder. Jon plunged his hand into the space between the seat and the back. "Damn, where are you?" he said to the couch. He moved his hand from right to left and back again, plunging it ever deeper. Then he did it again. "Wait," he said. "Bring me a knife. Doesn't have to be very sharp."

Barbie ran to the kitchen drawers and rifled through them. "Oh Mrs. Lee, where are you?"

Georgia stood in the center of the room, staring at her phone and listening to the slightly delayed ring from the sofa. Jon took a simple serrated edge knife from Barbie and swiftly inserted it under a thin line of neat handmade stitches not far from the corner. When he had ripped most of the threads out, grunting as he did so, he quickly retrieved the small cell phone. The machine continued to 'brinnnng' as he pushed the 'talk' button.

He turned, grinning at Georgia. "Hello!" he said.

Chapter Five: The Phone

Jon hung up the phone and handed it to Georgia.

She took it and stared at the tiny old-fashioned screen, a miniscule box compared to the modern iPhone.

"Contacts," Barbie suggested. "Maybe there are numbers on that phone of people you don't know, but he did."

"Right," Georgia answered, shaking her head as if to clear it of gathering cobwebs. "Where are the contacts?" she said, punching various buttons. "Wow, here we are. Some numbers, not many, but I'm there."

"We could call them," suggested Jon.

"Wait a minute, little man. Are you crazy? A phone, hidden away and we are just going to start dialing?" Barbie raised her voice. "Georgia, who are the other people? Do you know them?"

"The contact names are weird, no full names. Here's 'geo', that must be me because that's my number. Okay, let me start at the beginning, "'Bru.' Bru, bru, bru, Bruce Lee!" Georgia announced gleefully.

"Bruce Lee?" Jon repeated. "He's dead."

"Oh no, he's not. He's a breathing, walking, talking reincarnation. I've met him. Remember me telling you about someone who sold fake aphrodisiacs in Geylang, in the red-light district? Well, that's Bruce Lee. And he really looks like him, eerie."

Barbie took out her notebook and turned to a new page. "Let's have his number, just in case we want to call him on a different phone."

Georgia read off the phone number and then scrolled down. "'Geo,' that's me and then here is 'li.' Li, I don't know any Li's."

"Or it could be any one of hundreds of other Lee's, or Li's. It's a really common Chinese name." Jon said.

"Li or Lee. Maybe that's his landlady, Mrs. Lee." Georgia said. "I certainly don't have her number, so that might be good to know." She read it off and Barbie copied it down under 'Li or Lee."

"Next one?" Barbie asked.

"Wu," Georgia answered, "and I think that is our calligraphy teacher. I'll check my phone." She took her phone, punched and scrolled. "That's weird. My phone number for Wu is exactly the same except for the final digit, which is one off. I wonder if I got it wrong, or if this is wrong?"

"Is your number an office phone or a home phone?" Barbie asked.

"I don't know. I don't think I've ever called. It was just one night and Matt asked Mr. Wu for his number and we both took it down and put it in our phones. Maybe it was for asking about an exhibition or something. I just took it because Matt did." Georgia looked at the numbers again.

"Maybe it is an office phone. You know, some companies get a string of numbers," Jon suggested. "He could have one that was more work related, and another that was a bit more private."

Both Georgia and Barbie looked askance at this suggestion.

"Or something like that. Just suggesting," Jon mumbled.

"Thanks for helping. That's a possibility," Barbie said.

"At this point," Georgia added, "Everything is possible. Okay, on to the next one, 'xlu.' And here's the number."

Georgia read out the number and Barbie carefully copied it, repeating after Georgia.

"So, whose number is this?" Barbie asked.

"I HAVE NO IDEA," Georgia wailed. "This so frustrating. Numbers of people I don't know. What good is this doing us?"

"What else do we have?" Barbie asked. "The numbers, Georgia, just give me the numbers."

"How is that spelled again? X L U?" Jon asked.

"Yes," mumbled Georgia. "That's not even a name like Li."

"Well, maybe it is. Lu is a common surname in Chinese and X is a more common letter for a name in Chinese, unlike English. How many people do you know whose names start with X in English? Xavier? But in Chinese, there are lots. So maybe it's 'Something' Lu. Know anyone named Lu?" Jon asked.

Georgia made a face while concentrating. "No, can't think of any. But of course, I didn't know all his acquaintances." She looked at Jon pointedly. "How come you know so much about Chinese?"

"He studied it in college," Barbie answered with a proud glance at her son.

"And I've just spent two months in China, speaking and brushing up on it. But X Lu? Lu is a surname…"

"So, it has to be Lu Something," continued Georgia. "Surnames in Chinese always come first."

"Right," Jon said. "So, the X might stand for something else. Ten, as in Roman numerals? Or…?"

"Okay, okay. We got that one, we'll figure the rest out later. Next one," demanded Barbie.

"'Ys.' I know that one. Yannis," said Georgia.

"Ys is Yannis. Okay Georgia, if you say so. Spelled Y-A-N-N-I? And the number?" Barbie wrote it down.

"Yes, Yannis. But you need an 's' on the end. And his last name is St…… Or Sa….. He's Greek and its one of those impossible to pronounce names. So, we always just called him

Yannis. I told you about him, he's the one who was with us the day we took photos. He took the one of the two of us."

"So, this 'ys' is Matt's friend Yannis, who took the photo? Number?" Barbie wrote it down as Georgia read it out. "Maybe you could call him?"

Georgia answered slowly. "I don't know. I don't know him very well. And of course, I don't have his phone number. How can I explain that I got it off of Matt's dicey phone? The one hidden in the couch?"

"You don't tell him that," Barbie said.

"But what if he asks?" Georgia countered.

"Hey, leave it for now. Any other numbers?" Barbie turned back to her notebook.

"Yeah. Here's a great one. 'Z.' Just Z," Georgia answered as she read off the number. "Whoa, that's weird. Singapore numbers are always eight digits. This has only seven."

"Maybe it's a foreign number?" Jon interjected.

"But from where? It's not a complete number, just those seven numbers. If it's foreign, it needs an international number, at the very least," Georgia answered.

"Maybe it's not a phone number. Maybe it's another kind of number, maybe he put it there to store the number. Like a lock number, or a post office box number, some sort of ID number, a PIN for his bank card? Oh, the possibilities!" Barbie said.

"Whoops, there it goes!" Georgia said. "Ran out of battery life."

"Did we get them all, all the numbers? We only have seven of them, if we include you as well. Seven doesn't seem like very many." Barbie answered.

Jon interjected, "Did he have a charger? He must have had. We can charge it back up and check. Where did he keep things like that?"

Georgia looked at the desk area and sighed. "I think he would have kept them near the desk. There's a plug there and it's an obvious place. That box?" she said pointing at a shallow box that rested precariously on the shelf above the fold down desktop.

Jon looked and then shook his head. "Maybe in the bedroom?" He left the small living room and went into the bedroom.

Georgia and Barbie could hear rustling noises and rolled their eyes at one another. "Only a guy can figure out where another guy leaves his equipment," Barbie said. "On another topic, why did Matt have another phone?"

"I had no idea he had another phone. One night he just said, 'Oh, I have another number just in case… Here, take it down.' It was late, I was fuzzy-headed and he didn't act like it was any big deal. And he didn't say, 'Oh, by the way, I have another phone and here is the number.' Just a simple, 'here's another number where you might reach me.' In fact, I think I thought it was a friend's phone number."

"Why did he sew it into the couch? That's a really strange thing to do. I guess he was hiding it. Or maybe he didn't sew it in there, someone else did. Maybe you are right, it is someone else's phone," Barbie said, pausing to think, chin in hand.

Georgia stood and stared at the phone in her hand. She clenched her hand around the small device and her jaws worked clenching and unclenching. Her lips moved noiselessly and then she whispered to the phone, as if it could give her answers. "Oh Matt, Matt. Where are you?" She stared at the blank screen. "Where have you gone? Why don't you speak to me?"

Barbie let Georgia take her moment with Matt's phone. So far, Georgia had been nonchalant about Matt's disappearance. I wonder if Georgia really cares? Maybe Georgia has been keeping feelings to herself? That devil-may-care attitude that she has adopted is a ruse to put off the horrible thought that Matt has gone and will not come back!

"Did someone ask if Matt sewed the phone in the couch? Look what I found," Jon said emerging from the bedroom. He held up a small needle with a single strand of thread dangling from it. "Unless someone else has been into his things, I mean deep into his underwear, he did it himself. Oh, by the way, I found the chargers. Two of them. One is for a fancy new phone, the standard kind of plug. And this one," he held up an antique charger with a huge box with the plug handing from it. "Here, I'll get it hooked up. Where's the phone?"

Georgia held out the phone and the two managed to put the phone jack into the phone. "That's a bit wonky. The male part isn't smooth and it didn't go in easily. I hope it works. Yeah, it does. See the little bars are moving." Georgia smiled at the charging phone as if it held answers.

"Let me show you where I found that phone," Jon said, taking the needle and thread with him. "Look, right here. Yep, the same thread. See, it's deep into the corner." He sat on the cushion-less couch and pointed to the corner. "Because the phone is so small, it was easy to put it far into the corner. And if you could get your hand down into the back, you could run it around, like I did, and still not feel this. Because the corner was sewn, a person couldn't get his or her hand down into the corner. If the phone hadn't been ringing, I'd never have noticed this. Clever, whoever did it."

"But it still doesn't answer the question, why? Why sew the phone into the couch?" Barbie asked.

"To hide it, obviously. But when?" Jon continued. "It's an old phone, presumably an old-style battery. No one could have expected that it would last long. So, when did he put it there? It couldn't have been too long ago. Maybe a couple of days?"

"When was the last time you talked with him?" Barbie turned to Georgia, who had remained silent through the 'couch' questions. "Could he have hidden it then? Or did he have to do it later?"

"It was less than four days ago. I guess that phone could have lasted all that time. It was still on when Jon took it out of the couch," Georgia said.

"But not much juice left," Jon added. "He must have meant for someone to find it because he left it on. Why sew a phone into the couch, but leave it on? If he just wanted to hide it, he would have turned it off. That way, only he, or someone he told about it, could have retrieved it. And he must have meant it to be found fairly quickly. Phones are notoriously prone to running out of battery life."

"If you use them a lot. If you don't use them at all, they can stay charged for a long time," Barbie pointed out. "A week, two maybe. But you never know, do you? There are so many factors."

"And it's an old one, with an old battery," Georgia said, turning to look at the phone sitting on the small table in the 'kitchen.'

Barbie followed her gaze and then sniffed the air. "Is that smoke I smell? Coming from that phone, that one with the bad connecting wire? The one you said looked wonky?"

Now all of them watched the small device on the table begin to smoke, and the acrid smell of burning plastic and wiring filled the atmosphere.

"Eeeeek," Barbie jumped up, not daring to take her eyes off the now sparking, fizzing, smoking phone.

Jon leaped to his feet and grabbed a small towel hanging on a peg in the kitchenette. He grabbed the phone with it, but dropped it with a shout. He then went to the plug and yanked on the cord, disengaging it from the wall socket.

The three stood and looked at the phone as the fire slowly extinguished itself. Barbie pulled herself away from the spectacle to head to the window, pulling the sash open and letting in humid air, hot and smelly. On the way back across the room, she nearly stumbled on the small fan that was the air conditioner booster and turned it to the highest setting. The rattle of the small fan competed with the traffic and human noises from outside.

Jon stared at the phone and using the dirty towel, pushed it around on the table, flipping it onto its back. "I hope you got everything you wanted off that phone because you are not getting anything else." He used the towel and turned it face up again. The plastic case was browned and bubbled like a well-done crème brulee.

"This is one fried phone."

Chapter Six: The Appointment

"I think I got them all. The Z would be last, wouldn't it?" Georgia continued to stare at the phone.

"I copied down six numbers, Z was the last, I got that one, and yours would be seven. Does that sound right?" Barbie asked anxiously.

"All of them, or not, that's what we have." Georgia sighed and headed to the couch. "What do we do now?" She picked up the couch cushions and put them back on the couch and then flopped down.

"It's up to you, Georgia. What do you think would be most productive?" Barbie asked. "We're here to help. Aren't we Jon?" She looked at her son to make sure that offering his help was okay with him. She saw that a small smile played on his mouth, one side slightly more turned up than the other. It was a lopsided smile she remembered from his childhood. It meant he was engaged, happy, ready to move on. Suddenly, she felt tired and wanted to flop on the couch as well. Barbie envied Jon's energy and enthusiasm.

"Call Yannis. I think, just think, that I know him well enough to ask for his help," Georgia said softly. "But I am not totally sure of him. What can I say? 'Where's Matt? I've misplaced my boyfriend. What have you done with him?'"

"Casual," suggested Barbie. "Just a light-hearted, 'Have you seen him around?' That way you can act as if you two had a lover's tiff and he wasn't speaking to you."

"What about the phone number? How do I explain how I got the phone number? Tell him?" Georgia asked.

"NO," came the simultaneous response from Barbie and Jon.

"That phone was hidden for a reason," Jon said. "You could have gotten the number from Matt at any time. Probably best not to tell him anything."

"Be coy, pretend to be ditzy," Barbie added.

Georgia laughed, "Advice from the master of ditzy! Okay. Here goes." She picked up her phone and dialed.

"It's ringing," she announced. "Here, I'll put it on speaker and we can all hear."

"I'm here, remember, if you need a gruff, masculine voice. Let him know you are not without protection," Jon said, coming closer to where Georgia sat on the couch. Barbie also moved closer and opened her notebook, ready to write notes or silently give advice by writing.

After six rings, the phone answered with a click. But no voice came out.

Cautiously, Georgia said, "Hello." She paused and then said, "Hello, Yannis?"

A gruff voice answered, "Yeah."

"It's Georgia, Matt's friend. Hi, how are you?"

"Yeah, hi," came the answer.

Barbie motioned to Georgia with rolling hand gestures and mouthed, "Keep talking..."

"Hi," Georgia continued. "How have you been? Long time no see. Well, not so long, I guess, not in the last few days. How have you been keeping yourself?"

Another pause reluctantly gave way to, "Okay. I'm okay."

"Hey, have you seen Matt around? I haven't heard from him in a couple of days. Have you? Have you seen him or has he called you?"

"No, I haven't. Don't know."

"Do you know anyone else I can ask? Any ideas? Other friends you might know of?"

"I can't talk right now. Meet me in an hour at the park gate," came the gruff voice from the phone.

"Park gate?" Georgia asked with a slight panic in her voice. "Which park? Which gate?"

"Four o'clock. You know the gate, where we took the photos." The phone clicked off.

"Yannis, Yannis. What?" Georgia spoke at the phone. "I've got to call him back!"

"Georgia. Do you know this park gate?" Barbie asked. "If you do, can we all go meet him there. You don't have to go alone. Or are you afraid?"

"No, that's fine, that's good. I'm not afraid of him. But yes, it would be good to go together. An hour from now, let's see; five minutes, ten, no change, yeah, we have about a half hour before we have to leave."

"Let's keep looking here for any more evidence of where he went or what he was doing. Papers, books, anything in the trash?" Barbie asked.

"He read a lot. Look," Georgia indicated the bookshelves.

Hundreds of books, magazines and stacks of papers lined the shelves. Some had been thrown onto the shelves, but others seemed to be placed there in an order. On the top most shelf sat the empty cereal bowl, and a series of small boxes. Barbie wandered closer to look at them. She then started a systematic search from the bottom.

"Chinese," she said. "I know, Jon, that you studied it, but to read it, like this?" She took one book out and opened it. Across the page ran rows and rows of tiny Chinese characters, their complex arms and legs standing, sitting and waving in all directions. Jon looked over Barbie's shoulder.

"Language textbooks are one thing, novels and more scientific books another. No, I couldn't read those. But maybe we could find someone?" Jon asked.

"He used to 'study' some of these," Georgia said. "He would underline in them and turn corners down. Those are the ones I think we want to look for. Maybe later we can go through the others. And the papers, notes that he took. His English was good and he would write things in English, but also in his other languages. If we found any notes he wrote… Here's one," she said, reaching over Barbie's head to pull down a heavy colorful picture book, 'Guidebook to Xinjiang.' She opened it and flipped through some of the pages. "See, this is what I mean," she said, showing Barbie underlining and notes in the margins. She snapped it shut and put it in her small backpack. "Look for more like that."

Barbie lifted herself up to the higher shelves with the English books and ran her finger along the spines of the books. "Oh, here's one I have heard of. 'Foreign Devils on the Silk Road.' Look, he's written in this one as well. Shall we take it?"

"Yeah, and look, National Geographics. I wonder where he got them? Just a few, some of them old. Yes, every one has a story about Xinjiang. That's where he's from. Oooo, sticky notes in them. Good, maybe they can give up their secrets?" She took a stack and handed them to Barbie. "Whoa, that's a lot, maybe we can get them another time."

Jon had been flipping through stacks of papers and sat down in dismay. "He's photocopied lots of things. A few have underlining, but he didn't seem to make any notes on these. 'Geology of the Takla Makan,' 'The Zunggarian Basin,' 'Archeological Treasures of Lop Nor.' Oh wait. Here it is. A list of all of these articles. We can find them again if we need to. Take the list, leave the rest."

"Here's one to take for sure, 'The Sinkiang Story.' He actually read parts of this to me!" Georgia said, putting another book into her bag.

"I'm going to look in the bedroom again. Pants pockets, jacket pockets, loose papers under the mattress, that sort of thing." Jon announced.

Barbie and Georgia continued rifling through books, magazines and papers in silence.

"Arabic?" Barbie suddenly asked. "Is this his handwriting?"

"I'm guessing it's Uyghur. Traditionally it was written in Arabic script. Yeah, I guess this is his, and wow, pages and pages of it. Some English in here, and Chinese. Yeah, let's definitely take that. I don't know anyone who could translate it, but it seems valuable." Georgia checked her watch and jumped up. "Whoops, time to get going. But I'm not forgetting this," she triumphantly held up a plastic tube, three inches in diameter, two and a half feet long with a carrying handle that looked like cheap colored shoestring.

"What's that? Why are you taking it?" Barbie asked, looking surprised.

"Calligraphy. This is the good stuff, the keepers. We can see what he was writing." She carefully stuck the tube down the side of her pack and was able to zip the top around it, so only a few inches stuck out.

"Look what I found," Jon said, emerging from the bedroom. In his hands were torn bits of paper, scrunched up post-it notes and some more calligraphy paper with tiny characters written in pencil. "Never know what they may tell us."

Georgia parceled the books, magazines and papers out among them. As she left, she looked longingly at the shelves. "I hope that Mrs. Lee doesn't come by and remove everything, just to be a witch," she said. "Wait," she called out. Jon and Barbie were already out the door and did not see what Georgia went back to get. She came out empty-handed, but zipping up the outside pocket of her pack. She took out her key and locked the door from the outside.

They walked single-file down the narrow staircase and once more emerged into the bustle of Chinatown. Some stalls had already opened for business and the attendants were crying out their wares. Barbie could smell the aroma of frying garlic and chile as other stalls began cooking for the evening crowd.

The bustle and noise were infectious as Jon threw back his head, "Re nao," he proclaimed. "The Chinese have two words for noisy, 're nao' means 'happy noise', like restaurants with patrons talking, smacking their lips, belching, slurping their soup. The other word for noisy is 'chao nao', dirty noise. Loud cars, barking dogs, angry arguments; those are 'chao nao'. This is definitely 're nao'. Happy campers!" His pace picked up as he plunged into the crowds and happy noise of Chinatown preparing for Chinese New Year.

"This way, Jon," called Georgia as the group pushed their way through the scrum at the entrance to the Chinatown MRT station.

On the train, Georgia and Barbie managed to get seats together by barging and pushing their way in first to the last car of the train. Jon stood, hanging nonchalantly on a strap, swaying with the movement. The train ride was short and direct, but Georgia led them all on a merry meandering walk out of Dhoby Ghaut Station. They exited the station at the farthest end, walked across the lawn, and finally hugged the wall as it curved around a hill that towered over them. A tunnel beckoned them up into it and up the hill in a series of curving walkways. A road appeared, but no traffic stopped them as they slowly crossed it. A remodeled barracks building loomed on their right and ahead was a sign, 'The Battle Box.' Georgia veered to the right of it and took a path that sloped gently uphill. Lush vegetation grew on both sides of the path, monstrous green leaves seemed to grow even as they walked past, towering trees with hanging vines threatened to loop down and snag them, beds of intensely colored flowers sang with insect life.

"I'll bet this is spooky at night," whispered Barbie. "It's deserted now, must be even lonelier at night. Doesn't look well-lit."

"Oh," Georgia said, braking to an abrupt halt. "The Battle Box."

"The sign said it was the other way," Jon said.

Georgia approached a rusted metal door that was built into the rock wall, almost hidden in the dense foliage. "This is the back entrance, or rather the exit. I wonder if..." She reached out to the door that was adorned with an ominous sign 'NO ENTRY.' "Locked. I wonder if we could somehow break the lock or..."

At that moment, a noise came from behind the door, metal scraping on metal, and the old door creaked open. A clean-cut young Chinese man, dressed in a white shirt, tie and dark slacks, emerged. He stopped directly in front of Georgia. "Excuse me, may I help you?" He stepped forward, forcing Georgia to step back. From behind him, a line of tourists emerged, dressed in appropriate Singaporean touring costume.

"I want to go inside," Georgia said, trying to move forward and into the depths of the cave behind.

"I'm sorry, but our tour has ended. You need to come back tomorrow and go with a guide," the young man answered, with a set to his jaw.

"Just for a minute, I need to find something," Georgia insisted, trying to move around the young tour guide.

An arm sprang out and blocked her way. A gleam came into his eyes, which locked onto Georgia's. "You can come back tomorrow."

Even though Georgia had at least five inches on the young man, the vibes that emanated from him halted her advance. Barbie pulled on her arm and said quietly, "Later, Georgia, we can come back tomorrow if we want." Louder, she said to the man. "Thanks, we'll do that. Bye."

Back on the path and heading away from the Battle Box door, Barbie asked, "What was that all about?"

Georgia looked back and Barbie followed her gaze. The guide had a key and was locking the door, counting his charges to make sure he hadn't locked any away for the night. He cast a frowning glance at Georgia, seeming to dare her to try again.

"He told you," Jon snickered. "What were you going to do? Deck him?"

"Don't ever mess with a young Singaporean man. They ALL go into the army for 18 months, mandatory military service. And because Singapore isn't at war with anyone, they have nothing to do all day long, every day, but work out, and train to be tough guys. And the buffest young men that I've ever…"

"Georgia, enough of that. Why did you want to go in there? What is it?" Barbie pushed Georgia forward.

"It's the old military headquarters from WWII, built inside the hill, a good place to hide and be safe in case of bombing. It's where the British command headquarters were when they made the decision to surrender Singapore without a shot. Then it was taken over by the Japanese. After the war, they shut it up, bad memories and all, and a few years ago they opened it as a little museum. Matt took me there once. The whole time we were inside, he kept making jokes about hiding out, staying after they locked up. He said that it was a great place to disappear into because there were so many little corridors and rooms off in the dark where no one can see. He was fascinated with that kind of thing. Hiding." She stopped and looked around her. "I just thought that he may have taken off and hidden inside there. It was worth a try, at least."

"If you really think he's in there, we can go back and see if they will open it up. Or we can come back tomorrow morning," Barbie urged.

"No, I don't really think he's in there. I don't know where he is." She sighed, frustration edging her words. "Let's go find Yannis. The gate is just up here. This place, this hill, has been a palace and fort for hundreds of years. The British built the governor's house here, and then turned it into Fort Canning. Now it's a park. There's a reservoir on the top of the hill, important water supply for downtown Singapore, and some archeological digs, the burial place for the last Malay king of Singapore and this." She indicated the moss-covered stone wall with a deep opening in it that stood in front of them.

It looked ancient, as if it had been standing in this place for a thousand years, collecting small plants that grew from its cracks, and soot from a thousand campfires. In reality, it was only 150 years old, built by the British. It was one of the few remaining pieces of the wall of the fort, and had been maintained as a relic of an earlier time, part of the short British history of Singapore. The rounded entrance gate was deep in shadow, inscrutable and foreboding.

Barbie glimpsed to either side of the structure and when she looked back, a young man stood in front of them. He had mysteriously appeared when she had glanced away. Georgia was smiling and calling his name, "Yannis" as she moved towards him. Then he grinned and Barbie stumbled with shock.

He was tall, over six feet, with jet black, wavy hair, finger combed back in a haphazard mop. He was dressed in Singapore casual, his taut muscles standing out as he walked with a controlled cat-like motion. When he smiled, white teeth emerged from under a thick black mustache. At first Barbie had trouble breathing as her thoughts ran backwards to that other man in Cairo who so resembled the concrete, living man before her. She forced herself to breathe, gulping air and telling herself to put visions of the handsome antiquities dealer of the Khan el Khalili behind her. She mouthed the post office box number he had left with her as one of the few mementoes of their acquaintance. She had never heard from him after he left her in the Siwa Oasis, even though she had written dozens of postcards. "This isn't him," she whispered, even as the uncanny resemblance struck her again.

"Hey Mom," Jon called from behind her, "look at that!"

Startled from her reverie, Barbie turned to look at the object Jon pointed to. A light pole, towering above the majestic trees, had an extra-large light fixture. Immediately below it was mounted a long tube, the size of a small cannon, but obviously a camera lens. It pointed directly at her.

"Smile, you're on candid camera!" Jon crowed in delight at his discovery.

Chapter Seven: At the Gate

Barbie turned to watch Yannis plant two wet kisses on either of Georgia's cheeks. She had turned her face up to his, but then dropped it as she blushed at his familiarity. She beckoned to Barbie and Jon. "This is Matt's friend Yannis. My friend Barbie and her son Jon."

Barbie extended her hand, but instead of shaking it, Yannis took it in both of his, turned it over, bent over slowly and planted a sloppy wet kiss from his full lips on it. Barbie giggled. She tried to recall if anyone had ever kissed her hand upon meeting her before this. She eyed Yannis carefully as he took Jon's outstretched hand and pumped it firmly, adding his left hand to the right hand that grasped his. Jon returned the favor, and smiled warmly at him. Barbie felt they all now shared a warm, fuzzy camaraderie with Yannis.

"Come," Yannis said to them, "here out of the sun." He pulled them all into the deep shade thrown by the stone wall. They were the only people around. "Yes, lovely to meet you all. Now, what can I do for you, Georgia, my good friend?"

Georgia hesitated then. "It's Matt."

"Yes, you wanted to know if I had seen him. The answer is 'no', not for a week. So…?"

Georgia sighed deeply, then plunged ahead. "You see, he's gone missing. I think. I haven't heard from him and he usually calls me. So, I think he is missing."

"Did he tell you he was going out of town? You know, he often has business elsewhere," Yannis asked. "Have you been to his apartment?"

"Yes, I pounded on his door, but there was no answer." Georgia said with wide-eyed innocence.

Barbie started to open her mouth, but noticed a quick severe look from Georgia with a hint of head wiggle. She then understood the game that her red-haired friend was playing. Georgia did say that she 'thought' she could trust him, but Barbie realized that Georgia was not saying much, just as Yannis was not saying much.

"Did you knock really hard?" Yannis continued.

"To wake the dead! But, no noise from inside."

"Did you call him?" Yannis cocked his head. "Of course, you said. Do you mind if I try?" Yannis pulled a phone out of his pocket and swiftly punched in something. The four of them fell silent as they strained to hear the phone ring. Three rings later, the beep, beep, beep sounded to indicate that the phone number was not connected or out of service. "Ah, no answer. But maybe the other number, have you tried it?"

"What other number?" Georgia asked, her eyes wide in innocence.

"A few months ago, he gave me another number. He said it was an alternative. I don't know why."

"Oh, what number is that? I can try, just give it to me," Georgia chirped confidently.

"It may or may not be a good one. I'll try," Yannis said slowly.

Three pairs of eyes tried to lean in to see Yannis find the number. Three pair of ears tried to listen to the 'tune' of the numbers as they were dialed. But Yannis discreetly shaded the phone from prying eyes and coughed loudly as the numbers 'sang'.

Barbie leaned back and whispered to Jon, "I wonder what a fried phone sounds like?"

They all heard the beep, beep, beep signal of the unconnected phone line. Yannis shrugged. "That's no good either."

There was a collective sigh as they looked at one another, then finally, all eyes swiveled to Yannis.

Georgia bit her lip in frustration and began again. "Well, when did you last see him, exactly?"

Yannis shrugged. "Maybe you have seen him since I have? When did you last see him?" Yannis answered.

"Tuesday, at calligraphy class," Georgia answered.

"Ah, then you have seen him more recently than I have. There it is." Yannis grinned at his quick answer.

Georgia tilted her head to one side and narrowed her eyes. "Was he acting differently, the last time you saw him? Did he have some other business? For instance, do you think he had another girlfriend?" Georgia looked at Yannis with the injured look of a betrayed woman.

"Oh, no, no, no. I never saw him with another woman. I am sure you were the only one. Always the One. No, he seemed fine to me."

"What about his other friends?" Georgia pushed.

"I don't know his other friends," answered Yannis quickly.

"You know Bruce Lee, don't you?" Georgia asked just as swiftly.

Now, Yannis hesitated and a strange look came into his eyes. Barbie watched him carefully.

"Yes, I know Bruce Lee. But I don't know that Matt knew him very well. They weren't good friends, I'm sure." Yannis stared at Georgia, a defiant look that dared her to contradict him.

"Can you give me his phone number?" Georgia asked. "I'll call and ask him."

"I don't seem to have a number for him," Yannis said as he pretended to scroll through his contact list. "I'll tell him to call you, if I see him in the dojo. How is that?"

"The what?" Georgia asked.

"The dojo, martial arts clubhouse. That's where I met him. I see him there sometimes. I'm not sure Matt even knows where the dojo is." He said this with a surprised look on his face, smiling slightly at Georgia.

Jon stepped forward at this point. "You have a dojo here?"

"Are we talking about the same person, Bruce Lee?" Georgia asked, ignoring Jon's interruption. "The one that looks like the real Bruce Lee, always dresses in black?"

"The same." Yannis turned to the eager Jon and smiled. "Yes, of course we have a dojo here, many in fact. They are everywhere, man."

"Maybe I could come and visit sometime? Do some workouts? Just hang out. I know that usually you need some sort of introduction…"

"No problem. What do you do? Judo, karate…?"

"A little of everything. I studied at Shaolin for a while. Just really, you know, an amateur…" Jon seemed more hesitant now.

Barbie laughed to herself. She knew her son. He had done martial arts in high school and dabbled in college. But once he started something, he never stopped halfway, he always went full steam to the end. He was probably a black belt in something by now. Just an amateur? Not my son.

"Well, give me a call. Georgia can give you my number." He smiled at all of them, then turned. "I've got to go. See you later." He waved and turned to walk through the archway at the rear of the gate.

"Wait," called out Georgia.

But he had disappeared as easily and quickly as he had appeared. It was as if the shadow of the gateway had sucked him into itself.

Barbie moved out into the sunlight and stared at the archway beyond the shadowed wall they had chatted near. She saw nothing. "Where did he go?" she asked Jon and Georgia. "Did you see him go?"

"Wait, wait," Georgia wailed. She turned to Barbie and Jon. "He didn't tell me anything. Nothing! He didn't say when and where he had seen him, he didn't give me any phone numbers. How could he do that to me?"

"You didn't give him anything either, did you?" Jon pointed out diplomatically.

"Yeah," added Barbie. "You didn't tell him about going into Matt's apartment, and finding the phone. And finding the phone numbers."

"It was none of his business," Georgia declared. "He didn't need to know that."

"Maybe he thought Bruce Lee's phone number and the last time he saw him were none of your business," Barbie retorted.

"If you want to get information, you usually have to give some," Jon pointed out.

Barbie stepped back out into the sunlight and looked around. She walked out further into the open space in front of the arch and looked up at the camera again. She walked back to where they had been conversing and again moved out into the sunshine.

Georgia asked, "Barbie what are you doing?"

"Looking at the camera. It's a big one, isn't it? I mean, really big?"

Georgia looked up at the small cannon camera on the light post. "It IS big. Bigger than others."

"Others? You mean there are others? Are they everywhere?" Barbie asked.

"Ubiquitous." Georgia laughed. "Did I really use that big word? Everywhere. But I'm not surprised that this one is big. This is, after all, a militarily sensitive area. The water supply, the fact that it's a hill in the middle of the city. See the sign posts?" Georgia pointed to a nearby sign.

Barbie moved closer. It was in three languages, starting in English, then Chinese and some other language written in a Roman script. The warning was clear, no trespassing. A simple silhouetted picture of a soldier with a gun at the ready emphasized the message. She backed off.

"Are there any other cameras around here?" she asked, peeking into the trees and around the back side of the stone wall. "Do you see any Jon? You have good eyesight."

"I don't see any on the trees, and there isn't much else to put them on," he answered.

"They wouldn't be on the trees, would they? Tree leaves in the tropics grow very, very fast and they would have to be continually trimming the trees to make sure the cameras caught anything. That's why the light post is a good place. No foliage around to grow and obscure the images." Georgia laughed. "Why are you so interested in cameras?"

"That one, only that one around?" Barbie pointed at it. "It's big, probably has a really good quality lens in it, can capture anything, even in the dark. And I'm sure it caught us as we approached and while we've been standing here. Jon spotted it. But there is a curious thing about all of this."

"Curious? How? That there is a camera here?" Georgia asked.

"No, not the camera, just what it captured, who it took pictures of. As I said, it caught all of us, the three of us. We walked up there," Barbie pointed to the path that passed by the back door of the Battle Box. "And then we walked up here," she pointed to the spot where they stood. "All of it. But Yannis stood over there," she pointed to the archway. "He didn't come out here. He never moved out of the angle of the wall. The camera couldn't see him. It was as if only the three of us had a conversation here. Like Yannis was never here at all."

Chapter Eight: A Visit to the Calligraphy Centre

Georgia looked around, shrugged and said, "Let's go. Another person listed on that phone with a number was Mr. Wu, our calligraphy teacher. I'm not sure he'll be at the Calligraphy School today, but maybe the secretaries can help with the discrepancy in the phone numbers. At least it's worth a try." She set off purposefully back the way they came. "And Mr. Wu is someone I know I can trust. I'm not so sure about Yannis."

Jon jogged alongside Georgia, who was in high speed mode. "Do you mind if I go to the dojo? It wouldn't bother you?" he asked. "I'd really like to see what they do here in Singapore."

"I guess I don't care if you go. Oh, I don't know anything anymore. What I do know is that Matt is missing, truly missing. And I don't trust Yannis. But I guess it's okay." Georgia shook her head in frustration.

In one minute, they had arrived at the door set in the stone wall and hidden among the vines. Georgia saw it and veered off towards it. Barbie tried to hook her arm and prevent her from giving the door another rattle, when Georgia did just that, pulled and rattled at the door of the Battle Box exit.

"We can come back tomorrow," Barbie reiterated.

"I know, I know, it's just that he talked about this place. Well, he talked about a lot of places, come to think of it. He talked about so many things, all over the place and non-sequentially. It was as if his mind were a sieve, always finding and processing facts, or hypotheses, discarding some, manipulating others, just higgledy-piggledy. I never knew if what he was talking about was true or not, or exaggerated, or just flat made up." She released the door knob and headed back down the hill.

They got on the MRT and got off quickly at City Hall. As they came up the long escalator, they met crowds. People hurried in all directions, clutching packages, bags, backpacks, and most of them held a phone. Barbie took a deep breath and plunged into the maelstrom after Georgia. Jon followed behind the two women, using his height to gain a view. Georgia had obviously been here before as she rushed through the crowds, taking one turn after another in the vast shopping center. They passed a Starbucks and then a series of name brand stores. Small stalls had been erected in the center courtyards, selling items for Chinese New Year's. Barbie's eyes swiveled towards the goods laid out on tables and in display cases. The sounds of rushing water mixed with the sounds of rushing people.

Jon came up behind Barbie and laughed in her ear. "'City Hall' and it's a shopping center. I think that says something about the crazy world of Singapore. Is shopping the national pastime?"

"I think studying is, actually. But look at this stuff, much better than in Chinatown," she said.

"Oh, oh. There she goes," Jon said, grabbing his mother's arm and dragging her after the rapidly disappearing Georgia.

Soon they were outside, and the crowds thinned marginally. Georgia headed for the corner and crossed with the light, Barbie and Jon rushing to catch up with her. On the opposite side of the street, they passed a small entrance, with steps down into a large courtyard. Along the sidewalk in front of them, a long wall stretched out, stucco painted white.

"Former convent," Georgia announced. "Now…"

"A shopping mall?" Barbie supplied.

"Bingo! Also, restaurants and bars. But they have maintained the baby gate. It was also a school and orphanage and they had a little two-way door where you could leave your 'unwanted babies' for the nuns to take in. Singaporeans are like that. They love keeping their little treasures, but they tear down, dig up or transform anything in the way of their commercialization of the landscape," Georgia snorted.

Across the street, Barbie noticed some of Singapore's newer high-rises that housed banks and insurance companies. They were tall, multi-storied buildings with magnificent marble and stainless-steel lobbies. Grand entryways led up to doors offset to block the breezes while fountains played inside and out. Georgia assured them they were all 'feng-shuied' before being finished. "No one would dare try to rent out space in a building that wasn't aligned properly. 'Feng shui' masters make mucho bucks here, making sure 'wind' and 'water' keep in the money and keep out the bad influences."

Soon, they crossed the street again and Georgia led them through another colonial era building. Gracious thick white arches created a deeply shaded walkway that curved around a small parking lot. "Don't tell me," Jon asked, "Shopping?"

Georgia laughed. "Formerly St. Joseph's School and now the Modern Art Museum. They do some things right," she said, whisking them through another opening on the opposite side from where they had entered.

Barbie spied a street sign, 'Waterloo Street.' Georgia jaywalked across this much narrower street, passed the white synagogue with a prominent Star of David on the front, and then turned into the next courtyard.

As Barbie entered behind Georgia, she read the sign, 'Singapore Calligraphy Centre,' with the British spelling of 'center.' Looking up, she saw a two-story cream-colored building in the colonial style with tall green shutters. Sitting on either side of the massive metal studded double doors, were two stylized stone lions in the Chinese style. "Wow, another old building?" she asked.

"Actually, it's not," Georgia answered. "They built it to look 'colonial' and 'Chinese' at the same time, about 30 years ago. I like its ersatz pretentions."

"Big words again," Jon noted quietly. Georgia ignored him.

They plunged into the dark doorway. To the right as they entered, a woman sat behind a glass window. Georgia waved and they proceeded down the hallway. "They know me here, all of them. And they never forget the red hair." Turning to the left, she continued. "Notice that we don't go directly into the building. Jog a little, no direct lines. It's a feng shui thing."

Out in the courtyard in the back, they came across a group of teenaged students, all dressed in crisp white shirts and blouses and dark colored pants and skirts. They all carried large black portfolios and plastic tubes like the one that Georgia had retrieved from Matt's apartment. Barbie noted that all were Chinese, which by now seemed strange in Singapore. Silly, this is a Chinese calligraphy school. It would be strange if they weren't Chinese. But then she saw Georgia, and wondered again at the incongruousness of her friend's interest in this art form.

"Wu Lao Shi," Georgia said enthusiastically to an older man who stood just beyond the open classroom door numbered '2'.

He stood very still as the young students scrambled into the room. He wore a dark gray 'suit' of loose trousers and shirt that hung down. The top had a collar that stood up and was closed by a tiny ornately twisted frog closure made from the same material as the shirt. Barbie noted the texture and sheen. Probably silk. He wore frameless glasses with gold temples and had combed his thin hair across his head, leaving a high domed forehead. The image he exuded was elegant, old-fashioned, and non-apologetic for being so.

"Ah, my very best foreign student," he said with a slight accent. "Ni hao ma?"

Georgia looked to the sky as if seeking the answer in the clouds. "Ah," she finally responded. "Hao, hen hao. Ni ne?" She laughed, "And that's the best and last of my Chinese."

"Yes, yes of course," Teacher Wu responded. "But this isn't your class, is it?" He indicated the students who had now managed to straggle into the classroom.

"No, it's not. I wanted to ask you a question, and I thought you might be here. I wanted to know if you had seen my friend, Matt?" Georgia asked in a low voice.

Teacher Wu looked confused.

"My Uyghur friend; his name is Ahmet," Georgia continued.

The old man cocked his head and contemplated Georgia. He was many inches shorter than Georgia, but he remained calm and assured, as Georgia became more flustered.

"You must remember him?" Georgia continued.

Slowly Teacher Wu answered, "Yes. He was with you this week in class, wasn't he? Both of you? Together, yes?"

"Yes," Georgia confirmed. "Have you seen him since then, for example, yesterday?" She looked wide-eyed at him.

"No," he answered softly. "I have not seen your friend Ahmet since class." He stared at her and waited.

Georgia looked at Barbie and Jon as if to ask for directions or what she should or could say next.

"He didn't come by here looking for anyone, did he? Any of his friends, for example?" she tried again.

"No, I haven't seen him, nor talked with him. Why do you ask?" he replied, looking directly at Georgia.

"I haven't seen him either. I thought maybe he had been here," Georgia continued.

"Oh, have you misplaced him?"

"No, oh no, not misplaced. I just wondered if maybe…"

"I'm sorry I can't help you. I must go to my students now. If you will excuse me?" he said quietly and bowed slightly to Georgia and turning, bowed to Barbie and Jon. He turned his back on them, and silently slowly proceeded into the classroom, closing the door behind him.

Georgia led the way back through the calligraphy center. She hung her head as she slowly walked through the dark hallway. Jon and Barbie looked carefully at the scrolls that lined the walls. Jon stopped to admire one large piece, a flamboyant single character done with verve and flourish. Barbie peered at a photograph of a group, some sitting and others standing, taken in front of the Calligraphy Centre. She recognized a much younger Wu on the upper row, in the last position. A very old man with a wispy beard sat front and center. Georgia did not wave at the receptionist as they left the center and stepped out into the courtyard. The sun hung lower in the sky and the tall buildings threw long shadows across the street and onto the pavement. The sky was still bright, but dusk threatened.

They stood in a small group of three in the middle of the courtyard, where four small cars took up most of the space.

"What did you make of that?" Barbie asked. "He didn't have anything to add, did he?"

"He remembered seeing us together. But that was the last time I saw Matt as well. So, what does that tell me?" Georgia moaned.

"He's lying," Jon said.

"What, what do you mean? How do you know?" Georgia asked, startled at this pronouncement.

"All you had to do was look at him. Look at his eyes. He was lying, that's all I know," Jon continued.

"He's right, you know. He was always very, very good at telling if someone was lying or not. I could never fool him, never. Jon knows. He was lying." Barbie sighed and looked at Georgia who stood in the parking lot with her mouth open.

Chapter Nine: The Bras Basah Complex

Georgia looked up and back at the center. Barbie followed her gaze and noted that the green shutters were tightly shut, like two large eyes not willing to give up any secrets. The door stood open, like the maw of a monster. Or was it welcoming? Or was it too, lying and deceitful?

"I don't know what to think," Georgia said. "I guess I just have to go with the flow."

With determination, she plunged across the street, neither looking for traffic nor expecting to find any cars or other vehicles coming. Barbie and Jon followed her; however, they carefully looked both ways for errant traffic. Vile looking drains ran down either side of the narrow street. As they were covered with only metal grates, the sewer smells had free range to emerge and pollute the air. Mother and son scuttled after Georgia as she zipped once more into a dubious looking space at the back of a building. It turned out to be yet another shopping center. When they reached the central section, Barbie stopped to look around. It had once been a modern shopping arcade, built approximately forty years before, and reflected its age. An escalator ascended to the next floor, its grooved wooden slats rattling and groaning as it crept upwards.

They stepped on and rode single file as the narrow escalator was only one person wide. Georgia pushed forward, walking up the steps until her way was blocked by a woman with her small son in tow. Georgia fidgeted and almost bowled the woman over at the top in her attempt to push her way through. There was hardly anyone around and Barbie sensed Georgia's frustration as she and Jon marched along behind.

At the top, Georgia turned and walked in the opposite direction, towards the front of the arcade where light poured in from a balcony. However, Georgia stopped in front of the wide windows of one shop. She cupped her hands and looked into the interior. "This is where we always bought paper, ink, brushes, all the things we needed for calligraphy class. They also put your work on scrolls for you, for a price of course. But Mr. Wu recommended it, so we always came here, rather than to other shops." She turned and indicated at least two others in the row behind her.

Barbie looked at the goods displayed in the window, which were so numerous as to block the view to the interior. Foremost was an enormous calligraphy brush, at least four feet long, with a round section at the end containing an enormous clump of long stringy hair resembling a horse's mane. "Heavens! How do you use that?" queried Barbie.

"Standing, I think," Jon answered. "I saw a video once."

Hanging in the window were smaller strips of paper containing Chinese characters, some of them red with gold ink, as well as the usual black on white or cream paper. A row of small stone troughs was displayed on a narrow shelf. The top part of some were carved with dragons or leaves or other nature motifs. Barbie looked at Georgia questioningly. "Ink stones," she answered. "See the grayish purple one, there." She pointed to a small one that was lighter in color and had a delicate swirl in the stone. "The very best quality. It keeps the ink cold, so is more valuable. That little one costs at least $100, maybe even more."

Barbie gasped in surprise. "Pricey hobby, isn't it?"

A triple row of multicolored square stones, set in pairs, sat next to the ink stones. Their tops were carved into dragons, lions or other objects. Jon sidled up to Barbie. "Those I know," he said. "They are for your signature. You have your name carved on the bottom and then you use red ink to stamp your work. Like this." Jon pointed to a square red blob of ink that was a reverse stamp, the Chinese characters in white, while the background was red. It appeared on the left side of the paper. "I had one made for me, while I was in China. It has my Chinese name on it. But these are beautiful, much nicer than mine, and much bigger."

In the meantime, Georgia continued to peer into the shop, moving along the window to see if she could get a better view of the inside. Barbie looked as well, and then saw a curtain twitch in the rear of the shop. A middle-aged woman appeared and stood behind the counter. She smiled at the three on the other side of the window. It was a subtle invitation to come in, but since they were foreigners, they were not expected to take up the offer. Most non-Chinese just looked. "I don't know her," Georgia said.

"But you said you bought everything here, isn't there someone you could ask?" Barbie persisted.

"I can't ask someone I don't know. Even if she knows Matt, what can she tell me?" Georgia responded. She turned away from the window reluctantly.

Before they left, Barbie turned to look again at the display of an art and a culture she knew nothing about. "Calligraphy and martial arts are twin arts," Jon said quietly beside her. "It's the discipline. Where you have one, you often find the other. Great martial artists are often great calligraphers. They say you need to concentrate, be precise and control everything. I don't know enough to say anything else."

Barbie turned and saw Georgia wandering off towards a large, bright store, an incongruous commercial establishment amidst all the small specialty shops. 'Popular Books' ran the lighted sign across the renovated storefront. Joining her at the window, they all looked inside the store. Barbie noticed the mother and child from the escalator browsing through school workbooks, the rows labeled by grade. They were mostly Math and English books and the rows seemed to stretch to the back of the store. A flight of stairs pointed to more upstairs.

"This is so different from children's book stores that we went to, isn't it, Jon?" Barbie asked, touching his arm with her shoulder in a friendly bump. "Can you imagine how you would have felt if this was all you got? Workbooks?"

"You mean no 'Jonathan Livingston Seagull'? he answered.

"Hey, that wasn't my idea," Barbie said, referring to the 'in' joke of Jonathan's name. "And that's the last thing I ever let him do to you until you left me for him." Bitterness filled Barbie's voice as she lowered it to a whisper. "Just you be thankful that the 'Seagull' part got left off your birth certificate."

"You mean, I really was named after a character in a book? And here, I thought it was just some sort of weird coincidence." Jon looked at his mother, a puzzled look on his face. "I didn't even know until much later that there was a book. Shows you how out of touch I was. Some girl asked me what the 'L' stood for, that's how I found out."

"I was okay with the Jonathan, why not? And the Livingstone was just silly. But I put my foot down on the Seagull. We parted over that, you know." Barbie said, slowly grinding her teeth.

"No, I didn't know. No one ever told me," Jon's voice held a whine.

"There are things you don't talk about with your children. You didn't need to know. And it's water under the bridge now."

"Oh, there you are," Georgia said, approaching them from the opposite side where they had last seen her.

"Where'd you go?" Barbie asked.

"I went down there," Georgia pointed to a row of small shops deeper into the arcade.

Barbie found herself walking in that direction as Georgia followed. "Where are you going?" Georgia asked. "No one is there. I knocked."

"Why did you knock? Who were you looking for?" Barbie asked, suddenly feeling left out of Georgia's search.

"Oh, sometimes he would come here, I don't know which shop he traded at, but he had small things from China to sell. See the sign?" Georgia pointed to the small signs that appeared on all the shops here. 'Chinese antiquities bought and sold.'

Barbie peered at the other signs, hand lettered or cheap prints made from a computer. She saw one, a large Chinese character, that she recognized. It was the same one that Matt had been practicing so hard, 'jin.' "What…"

"Downstairs," Georgia demanded. "I do know the guy downstairs at the bookshop. Let's go." She turned and headed towards the 'down' escalator which shared a space with the 'up', crossing halfway on their journeys.

Downstairs, they proceeded to a line of bins, piled high with books stuck neatly into boxes. They were sorted by size rather than subject matter, but it was a better method of displaying the vast number of used books on offer. The signs over the bins proclaimed their cheap price and quality. Georgia stood a moment looking up at the sign, 'Evernew Books.'

Sidling up to her, Barbie asked, "Going into this one?"

Georgia bit her lip in thought. "I don't really know him either. But Matt came here often. He used to order books from the bookstore owner, by the box load. Then he'd take most of them back. He was here a lot." The three walked into the store.

At first, no one was visible, so they spread out, each searching out a section of possibly interesting books. Barbie found a section of English books. The prices were triple what the cheap Chinese or faded old books at the entrance were, but they seemed to be current and in good condition. Because they were heavy on thrillers and classics, Barbie soon gave up and poked around looking for Jon and Georgia.

Above the bookshelves were displays of porcelain statues, some white and others painted in bright colors. They depicted 'heroes' of the revolution, the Communist revolution as Barbie soon realized by the posters also on display. The glorious young Mao Zedong looked out to the horizon, his arm raised in welcome, or a gesture to revolution. They were yellowed and faded, yet the bright red hammer and sickle still stood out.

Barbie spied Jon in a section containing language textbooks and dictionaries. "I don't know why I'm looking, I can't carry any of these anyway. I just use my trusty Kindle. Thanks Mom." Jon grinned at his mother.

Together they poked further into the store and found Georgia standing amidst a small disaster, stacks of books piled around her feet. "I knocked them over. He's going to hate me. Help me pick them up. It doesn't matter in what order, I'm sure."

They busied themselves stacking the books into neat, stable piles. When they were finished, Georgia poked her head around the corner and hissed at her fellow investigators. "He's there now. But I don't think I can ask him, either."

Jon looked at the owner and opined, "He looks a bit stupid, if you ask me. Sleepy-eyed, maybe he takes drugs??"

"I mean, Matt's my friend, I should know where he is," Georgia whispered. "Why did I think I could ever ask strangers about where he is? I mean, it's different with Yannis and Mr. Wu. I know them, I might even say I'm friendly with them. But this guy? I don't even know his name." She peeked out and looked at him again. "Come to think of it, I don't know why Matt came here. It's so out of character for him. He hates all this old-fashioned political propaganda."

"But isn't he, well, Chinese?" Barbie whispered.

"Yeah, he has a Chinese passport, but that doesn't make him Chinese, or like them very much. He is a minority." Georgia said.

Barbie watched Jon as he approached the store owner as he stood behind the counter. The man was immensely large, his white shirt opened to show a triangular tract of pale hairless chest. His eyes had grown small in the flesh of his face, while his lips had expanded to fill the lower half of his face. Greasy black hair was combed back, leaving a large sweep of prematurely balding forehead. His fat arms splayed away from his body as his pudgy hands supported him as he leaned on the wooden counter. Immobile, unflinching and seemingly unresponsive, the young man glared at Jon.

Barbie listened to the brief exchange. Jon asked how much the small book in his hand cost. The answer came back to Barbie garbled, but no matter what the price, she knew Jon wasn't buying. What is he up to?

"Thanks anyway," Jon said loudly as he turned back to Georgia with a question mark on his face. His mimed asking a question. Georgia shook her head wildly.

Barbie looked again at the clerk. Over his head hung a large poster of a mature Chairman Mao, the classic pose of a middle-aged man, his dark hair combed back, leaving a large bald spot.

"Do you think he's a communist? Are they allowed in Singapore?" Barbie whispered to Georgia.

"Oh, I don't think they would bother someone selling outdated Cultural Revolution souvenirs. Maybe he is a communist. But that's what's so strange about Matt. My Ahmet hates the Chinese government and communism. Hates. So why did he come here so often? And why did he buy books from this place? Who is this guy anyway?"

Barbie took one last look at the owner, the possible communist, as they trooped out the door. His eyes bored into hers. Barbie shivered under his gaze which seemed to mock her very existence.

Chapter Ten: Raffles Hotel

On the sidewalk, Barbie looked across the street. To the right sat a large complex of buildings, painted white with green and gold accents. Jon appeared to her right and looked questioning at the colonial style building. "Is that Raffles Hotel?"

They turned to Georgia, who joined them at the curb. "Yes," she answered. "And if you'd like to say you've eaten at Raffles, I know of a fairly cheap place. Any takers for a quick meal?"

Yes," Barbie and Jon answered together. "I'm ready for some food. Lunch seems like a loooong time ago," Barbie said.

"Soup restaurant, here we come," Georgia said as she led the way.

A short walk brought them past the rear of the square block of the hotel. A small circular drive allowed taxis and limousines to drop their passengers out of the rain and sunshine onto a wide sidewalk. Shops could be seen with discreet signage to both right and left. A wide staircase led to upper floors. Peeking into the interior courtyards, Barbie saw huge palm trees, trimmed bushes and flowering plants crowding into the red brick courtyards and marble lined walkways. Elegance, old-world charm and affluence oozed from the courtyards, balconies and boutiques.

Barbie absorbed the colonial atmosphere as she (mostly) tuned out Georgia's lecture about the Armenian Sarkies brothers who founded the original hotel in 1887, the famous tenants such as Somerset Maugham and the renovations in the late 1980's that added air-conditioning, causing room prices to soar. "You do know about the Singapore Sling, don't you Jon?" she asked. "I once referred to Matt as my 'Singapore Fling' and Barbie won't let me forget it." She laughed hollowly.

"Can we get a Singapore Sling? They still serve them, don't they?" Jon asked.

"Vile. Pink. Over the top sweet. Dubious liquor. You don't want one." Georgia turned her head. "If you really insist, we can stop by the Long Bar, crunch the peanut shells underneath and you can have a long beer, Tiger beer. But I think it's too touristy!"

At an inconspicuous doorway in the wall, they entered the Soup Restaurant. The waiter led them to a quiet corner booth, where they perused the menus. Barbie ordered chicken soup, Jon seafood soup and Georgia a vegetarian soup. As the waiter left, Barbie stood up and surveyed the restaurant. "We are alone here, we can talk."

"Talk?" Georgia asked. "About what?"

"The case," Jon filled in, "in order to understand and solve a case, you need to lay out the facts, the suppositions, what you know and what you don't. That's how classic detectives do it."

"I didn't know," Georgia answered.

"Well, we do. And you know, I've solved cases before. Now that I have my trusty sidekick with me, we can begin to get a grip on all this." Barbie took out the notebook that she had used to jot down the phone numbers from the burnt phone.

"You have the phone numbers, we can start from there," Georgia suggested.

"No, we need to start from Matt's disappearance. The last time you saw him. That's our start time. You said that he had given you the key and the phone number earlier, so we need to leave a space for that, but it starts with the last time you saw him. That's where to start, isn't it 'boy detective extraordinaire'?" Barbie turned to smile at Jon. "You don't mind that I call you that, do you? You're hardly a boy anymore." She cocked her head to one side and smiled at Jon.

"You're right, I'm not a boy anymore, but I still like the detective bit. I think that studying law will be a good thing for me, I need grounding, depth, not just the pseudo excitement." Jon smiled back at his mother.

"You two are not kidding, are you," Georgia said, staring at the pair. "Boy detective!"

"So, shall we start while waiting for the soup?" Barbie began the questioning.

She left a few lines for dates and events before the 'last time seen' space, but made sure that Georgia filled her in on the time line. Georgia denied any contact, or any actions by herself or Matt, in the three days since she had seen him. So Barbie filled in the phone number transfer, unknown date because Georgia couldn't remember exactly when it was. "Before Christmas, that I know."

"And the key? The more precise the better," Barbie urged Georgia to remember.

Georgia looked into her bag and dragged out a small daily calendar. She flipped back through it, trying to relate other events with receiving the key. "All I can say is about a week ago."

"Let's just give it a date a week ago. I don't know if it's important or not. So, what have we got for today?" Barbie dutifully noted all the events in chronological order that happened on that day. "Nine o'clock, went to Matt's apartment. Found nothing."

"We found that his passport and computer were gone, so that's important." Georgia added.

"We'll put that under discoveries. Going to the airport to meet Jon, not important, back to the apartment. Meeting Mrs. Lee, oh, not paying the rent. That is important. And the big thing, the phone! And we have the phone numbers of a number of people. Right here. Some of them we know, Mrs. Lee, we think, Bruce Lee, Yannis, Mr. Wu, but there are others? We still don't know. And there is a note here about a discrepancy between Mr. Wu's phone number that you have and the one on the phone…"

"Oh no, I forgot to ask the receptionist about that. I guess we can go back." Georgia looked annoyed and checked her watch. "It's too late, she'll have left for the day. Now that is going to bother me until I can go back."

"Why don't you just call the other number?" Jon asked.

At that moment, the waiter appeared with three steaming bowls of soup. The detectives paused in their pursuit of justice and the missing boyfriend to eat for a few minutes. Georgia soon put her spoon down with a snort of annoyance. "I can't just call. How will I explain how I got that other number? Remember, we're keeping the phone and the numbers to ourselves for the time being. Aren't we?" Georgia suddenly sounded unsure.

"Of course, we are keeping a lot of information close to our chests. That hidden phone is weird, out of the ordinary, and so we will remain silent. What else do we have?" Barbie asked.

"Yannis was hiding something. Put that down," Jon added, pausing between slurps. "He didn't tell us anything and he was hiding something. I can try finding him in the dojo and confront him?"

Barbie gasped, "You will not! You will confront no one. This is about a missing boyfriend, not criminal intent. Let's keep this all in perspective! But I will put down that Yannis is not trustworthy."

"And also Mr. Wu. If Jon says he's lying, I guess we have to believe him. But I still don't know why." Georgia looked at the ceiling for inspiration and then went back to her soup.

They ate in silence for a few minutes.

"Who's Z? And Xlu? And why didn't you ask the bookstore owner about Matt?" Barbie pushed Georgia. "If you really want to find out, you have to ask."

"Put it up on Facebook. Then everyone will find out," Jon suggested.

"Yannis said he might be on a business trip," Barbie added. "And, I hate to bring this up again, but maybe he did run off with someone else? Could it possibly be?" whispered Barbie.

"Maybe. If he'd wanted to end it, I think he would have said," Georgia replied timidly. "Remember, he gave me the key to his apartment just a week ago. So, running off with someone else? Naw, doesn't compute."

"So what else do we have?" Jon asked. "Did you really ask Mr. Wu where Matt was? I mean, you asked if he had seen him, not if he knew where he was. Two different questions."

Georgia looked at Jon in puzzlement. "But the implication was that I hadn't seen him and I was looking for him and that if Mr. Wu knew where he was, that I wanted that information." She shook her head in frustration. "Leave it to a man to think that if a girlfriend comes asking about her boyfriend, that she really shouldn't be told, or that she's asked the wrong question. His English is very, very good and he knew very well what I was asking. I was trying to be subtle." Georgia ground her teeth in frustration.

Barbie banged her spoon against her bowl and slurped her soup. In a fake bright voice, she said, "Really, this is very good. Mine has ginger in it. How's yours, Georgia? This is a great little place. Thanks for the suggestion."

Georgia looked at Barbie and Jon and muttered, "Sorry Jon. I'm just frustrated. I didn't mean to take it out on you. And thanks Barbie. I come here often, it's a little bit of 'Ye Olde Singapore.'"

Jon muttered, "Just trying to help, didn't mean anything…"

They engaged in soup eating for a few minutes and then Georgia ventured, "So, Jon. Your name really is Jonathan Livingston, without the Seagull?"

"Yeah, really. And now my Mom has told me that it was the reason my parents broke up.

Barbie said laughingly, "You brought us together, you broke us apart."

"Hey, I wasn't around for any of that," Jon protested.

"Oh, yes you were. I mean, not when we first met, but…well…soon after…" Barbie said to Jon. She looked at his blank face and then fell silent. "You mean, no one ever told you?"

"Told me about what?" Jon asked, his face wearing a giant question mark.

"Why we got married?" Barbie said softly.

Jon's face registered a slow comprehension. "You mean, you were… with me?"

Barbie laughed, "Don't look so shocked. It's nothing new for heaven's sake. I just thought you might have figured it out by now, or that your grandmother or grandfather would have let something slip. They never let me forget it," Barbie said, her eyes glued to Jon's to gauge his reaction.

"And you broke up over my name?" Jon asked.

"It was a very short marriage, barely six months. But I had you." Barbie smiled at Jon affectionately.

"But I wasn't wanted?" Jon looked slightly frightened.

"Oh yes you were! I never, never ever thought about giving up on my baby, even when he asked."

"He asked you…to get an abortion?"

"He suggested it. I suggested marriage."

"And Grandpa got out his shotgun?"

"Something like that. You see, my parents only had the one kid and the thought of a grandchild, well, it was thrilling for them. No, no giving up on you. You might not have been planned, but you were definitely wanted." Barbie said.

Jon sat in silence and finished his soup.

Georgia had said nothing in all this and now leaned over to Barbie and whispered. "Any more revelations? Any other skeletons in the closet you want to dig up? Any more 'dirty laundry'?"

"Don't be melodramatic!" she whispered back. More loudly, she said, "I just want to say, for all to hear, that I am so happy and pleased that Jon, my wonderful son, is here with me now. We have managed to bungle every vacation; every opportunity has been missed until now. I'm sorry we haven't managed it, but now, we are here together. I am so…pleased." Tears sprang to Barbie's eyes and as she looked at Jon, she noticed little sparkles of water in the corners of his eyes as well.

"We never lost touch, never. Maybe physically not close, sometimes continents apart, but not separated when and where it really counted." Jon leaned into Barbie's shoulder in an intimate gesture of solidarity, comfort and connection. Barbie leaned back.

Georgia looked at them, sitting side by side, touching ever so slightly and smiled at them. "This thing," she gestured at the shoulder-touching, "what's it all about?"

"Boys can't hug their mothers, or kiss, or hug, or pretend even to care, can they?" Barbie said.

"So, this is the solution. Neat, isn't it? Most people never even noticed," Jon said, smiling at Georgia. "But she's shorter now than she used to be. We used to be almost shoulder to shoulder, now she's kind of short." Jon looked down affectionately at his mother, sitting much lower in the booth seat than him.

"It's good to finally see you too. I just wish that it could have been a little sooner. I just wish that you'd been able to come to…"

Abruptly, Georgia interrupted them. "Listen!" She looked at the two sitting across from her. "Oh, sorry to interrupt the reunion. But I think we need to go back to Matt's apartment. I am just sure we have missed something. Both times we were there, we didn't have a chance to really 'search' the place. We didn't really look!"

Barbie shook her head and looked up at Georgia. She had known Georgia as a fellow teacher in Turkey and had always been surprised at her ability to switch gears quickly. Yet one more time, topic to topic. Why can't she just make up her mind about something and do it? What's all this hither and yonning about? Hell, let's just go with it, what else do we have to do? "Okay," Barbie said, "let's go back and look again."

"We found the phone sewn into the couch, that's not looking?" Jon added.

"Yeah, yeah, yeah. That was a good Matt joke. He was always playing games, being secretive, planning these weird surprises. He loved puzzles. And he gave me a key. I know that there is more there. He knew I would come looking and he left clues for me, I'm sure of that now. I know there is more to find. We need to go back. We have to look again," she said, her voice becoming shakier and higher in pitch.

Barbie recognized the beginnings of a panic attack, but she felt helpless to do anything but go along with Georgia's whims. Maybe she'll settle down if we just humor her. "Okay, my fellow sleuths, we search again. Let's go."

Georgia's face drained of color and her eyes darted from side to side. A high-pitched whine keened from her throat.

Barbie stood and slipped into the seat beside her friend. "It's okay. We'll go. We're with you. We're here." She stroked Georgia's back until her friend relaxed.

Barbie caught Jon's eye as silent agreement passed between them. Georgia had finally acknowledged the seriousness of Matt's disappearance.

Chapter Eleven: Return to the Apartment in Chinatown

After quickly settling the bill, which Barbie insisting upon paying, they emerged onto the covered sidewalk. Georgia strode quickly, leading the way by retracing their steps. At the circular drive, she lifted her hand and a taxi appeared from nowhere, or at least from a location that Barbie couldn't see. As before, Jon sat in front, but Georgia gave directions. Within a few minutes, they were again in Chinatown, amid the crush of locals and now tourists visiting the four by four block square known for its old buildings. Georgia sped ahead and Jon held Barbie's hand as they struggled behind, trying to keep up with Georgia who was now in a full-blown panic mode. Within two minutes, they were once more in the alleyway and at the door that led to Matt's apartment.

Georgia fumbled with the key, cursing under her breath when the metal tongue failed to engage the lock. While Barbie tried to quiet and soothe Georgia, Jon fiddled with the key. Although it was only seconds, Georgia acted as if it took a lifetime to open the alleyway door. Dusk was rapidly falling and Barbie knew from experience that within minutes, it would be dark in this tropical zone. Georgia thanked Jon for unlocking the door, but then insisted upon having the key back so she could lock the door securely behind them. Silently but swiftly, they climbed the stairs. At the top, Georgia stopped and breathed deeply. The proximity to her goal seemed to have given her a new calmness.

"Maybe he's come back. Maybe all this worry was for nothing," Barbie said in hopeful tones. "Yes, that would be great. I can tell that you need to solve this. Here's for good luck." She crossed her fingers and held them up.

"I hope you are right," Georgia said as she once again fumbled with the keys, her hands shaking. She inched the door open.

Barbie looked over Georgia's shoulder. The window shades stood open, where they had left them, and light from the outside poured in. The floor appeared to be covered in white sheets. Georgia's hand snaked into the room to turn on the light.

The brilliant light hurt Barbie's eyes as she tried to see what was inside the room. She felt Jon jostle against her back as he pushed himself into the room. He stood in front of them and looked at the room, now lit by the overhead light.

Barbie saw that the 'sheet' was, in fact, sheets of paper. Someone had pulled the piles of photocopied papers off the shelves and strewn them on the floor. Every book had been snatched from its neat place and thrown on the floor, many of them open, adding to Barbie's initial vision of whiteness. She turned her head and looked at the small kitchenette in the corner. The few dishes and pots and pans had likewise been dislodged and lay dumped on the table and floor. A few glasses had been broken in the sink, making it a treacherous basin of sharp, barely visible shards.

Georgia had sucked in her breath as she perused the scene. She stood still, not daring to move into the apartment, or wade through the sea of papers.

Jon announced, "I'll check the bedroom." He walked easily through the papers, trying to disturb as little as possible and Barbie saw the light in the small room beyond go on. Within half a minute, it went off and he returned. "The same thing in the bedroom. Everything has been pulled out and dumped on the floor. The bed has been turned up and the sheets pulled off and wadded up. Even his underwear is strewn all over. Georgia," he turned to her and tried to get her attention as she stood still at the very edge of the chaos. "What's missing? What was taken?"

Barbie pushed Georgia forward a few inches and closed the door behind her. "Can you tell if anything is gone?" Barbie asked Georgia again.

"Oh God," she whispered as she put her hand out to find a chair to sit in. In the end, she leaned against the door and sunk to the ground. "Who did this? Why?"

"What were they looking for, Georgia?" Barbie asked.

Jon walked to the desk and once more looked into the drawers. "Nothing," he announced. "They are empty." He looked under some of the papers on the floor and picked up some of Matt's calligraphy brushes. He then wandered to the window and looked out. A moment later he leaped backwards.

Barbie squeaked in surprise, "Is something out there?"

Slowly, Jon leaned down and crept to the edge, pulling at the blinds, trying to close them. "I just realized that anyone outside could see in. We don't want that do we?" By pulling on the shade, he managed to block most of the view from the outside, but the shade had been damaged in the rampage that had occurred.

Jon bent to pick up some of the papers, but soon snorted in disgust. Barbie realized that whoever had scattered the content of the shelves had meant to confuse and 'destroy' their order. A notebook had its pages of notes ripped out and mingled with photocopies, magazine articles and newspapers. Jon began to stack them neatly, but soon abandoned the job. He went to the couch and with a great sweep of his long arm, brushed all the papers off the couch. Underneath, the couch cushions appeared, having been displaced as well. "Oh, look," he said, pointing to the corner of the couch where he had found the phone.

A round black hole gaped in the very end of the couch where the back met the seat. All around the hole was a disemboweled pile of pale stuffing, like a volcano of couch innards had erupted. Georgia pulled herself off the floor and gingerly walked across the room, trying not to step on any papers, and failing. She approached the couch and peered into the hole. She reached her hand out, gingerly touching the nearest bit of fluff. Then she slowly stuck her hand into the hole. It only went in a few inches and she pulled it out.

"How did they know where to look? You could hardly tell anything had been there and we put the covers back on. Why tear it all up like this? Was there something else in that couch? I knew we had to come back. I just knew that there was something else here," Georgia stood and faced the others.

"Maybe it was Matt?" Jon suggested.

"No, he'd never do anything like this to his own apartment. Maybe tear up a little bit of the couch looking for the phone, but not trashing it."

"No one in their right mind would do this to their own stuff," Barbie commented.

"Maybe he told someone about the phone," Jon said. "And they came in looking for it."

"Then why do all this? This is destruction. It was Mrs. Lee. She is the only one who has keys," Georgia said.

"Ever hear of lock picks? These are just ordinary locks." Jon's tone was mild as he made this statement, Barbie noticed.

"She shouldn't have done this. This is illegal. Even in Singapore, tenants have rights." Georgia continued.

"This is spooky," Barbie said. "It's like being violated. Personally. Someone breaks in and goes through your personal stuff and steals it. Rifles through your underwear and things. Jon, do you remember when someone broke into our house? They stole some costume jewelry…"

"And my little computer game. Yeah, I remember. Not nice, creepy," he said.

"Nothing valuable, but I did feel personally assaulted," Barbie said, "this feels the same."

Georgia pushed aside some papers and sat on the kitchen chair. "Who did this? Who? Who? Who?" she repeated angrily. "Where is Matt? Why this??"

Barbie could see that Georgia held back tears as she tried to control her anger. "Shall we help you clean this up? Maybe if things are neater, then you will feel better and if Matt comes back, then he won't have to come back to this terrible mess," Barbie offered, nodding her head at Jon to start picking up papers and putting books back on the shelves.

"Oh, I don't know. I guess so. It's hard to think what to do. I'm angry, I'm puzzled. I don't know what to do." Georgia slumped in the chair and absently began picking up papers off the table and putting them into a neat pile.

"You're tired, we all are," Barbie said. "Let's clean this up and then get some rest!"

Georgia was fiddling with a black cord that had been left on the table when her breath started becoming faster. "Oh no, oh God, oh no, not this, this can't be happening," muttered Georgia, her voice rising in pitch and tone. "We can't stay here, we have to get out. This is awful. Ahhhhh," she screamed and threw the small black string back onto the table.

Barbie rushed to her side and grabbed her arm. "Georgia, what's wrong? What's happened?"

Georgia threw her arm out and pointed at the short cord on the table.

Jon approached and looked carefully at it. "It's the cord from Matt's phone; the one we burnt trying to recharge it. Look, the end is burnt."

Georgia stood and pointed at it, her hand shaking. "Look, look at it. Turn off the light. Don't let anyone see us here. We have to leave. Now." She grabbed her pack from the floor and grabbed the keys. She checked briefly to make sure that the books and papers that she had rescued earlier that day were stowed inside. She brushed her hand against the plastic tube to make sure it was still there. "Quick, quick, we need to go. NOW." She reached for the light.

Jon held up the cord and just before the room went dark, Barbie saw it. It registered slowly as the reason for Georgia's panic. Georgia, now in full panic mode, began to moan and cry. "Don't let anyone know we were here. We have to go. We can't be seen."

Barbie grabbed her small pack as well, weighted down with books that she had been carrying all day. Jon came behind her and steadied her dash out the door. As she descended the now dark staircase, using both hands to guide her, the vision came back, now seared into her brain cells. The little black cord had been tied into a miniature hangman's noose.

Chapter Twelve: Searching for Clues

The three scurried down the stairs and quickly got out of the stairway into the alley. Dusk had fallen and the street lamps cast bright spots of light as well as shadows that crisscrossed the unevenly paved street. The alley was deserted and seemed even lonelier because the noise from the main street had become louder. Even though the holiday was three weeks away, shoppers had come out in force to get early bargains. Some hoped to snatch the chance to get the latest, the newest in kitchen gadgets or whatever would cause their neighbors to envy them.

In the alley, Barbie glanced up and down to see if she could find any cameras that might give away their location. She saw one as soon as they turned the corner, heading for the main street, but it pointed down into the milling crowd. Why would anyone be interested in the three of us, anyone who had access to security cameras, that is? Why should we be afraid? Barbie's thoughts came thick and fast as they raced towards the melee in the main street. She grabbed Georgia's arm to keep her from rushing ahead, but also to not lose her among the crush.

They quickly eased through the throng to the end of the street and braked to a halt at the taxi stand. A taxi stopped and Georgia pulled the door open even before the occupant could pay and gather her parcels. Barbie grabbed Georgia's arm and whispered to her, "Let the lady leave. Don't worry, we're here with you." She felt Georgia's shaking arm under her hand and moved closer, hoping the proximity would comfort her.

Before they were settled in the taxi, Georgia had croaked out the address. As they distanced themselves from Chinatown, Georgia became quieter and more subdued. At the apartment building, Barbie leaned forward to the driver and paid. She pushed Georgia out and quickly exited behind her. "Are you okay now?" she asked.

"Better, better, but…" Georgia looked all around her as the taxi drove away. She stared pointedly at a young man loitering near the corner of a building, but he moved swiftly after absorbing her stare. She continued her reconnaissance until satisfied and then she nodded to her compatriots to proceed.

Inside the apartment, Georgia threw herself on the couch and curled into a fetal position. "Someone was warning me. Someone knew I had been there," she declared.

"We were all there. All of us are in this together," Barbie answered and looked pointedly at Jon. "You are not alone."

Jon chimed in, "I'm here for you too."

"Thanks, both of you. And you are right, I know I'm not alone. And I really, really appreciate you being here with me. I think I was treating all of this as a joke. 'Where's Matt? Where's he gone?' But now," she paused. "I think something has happened to him. It's the cord, the cord to his phone." She shuddered visibly and then went on. "Someone is trying to tell me something. Telling me not to play around. It's a threat, a nasty childish threat!"

Barbie sat next to her and asked quietly, "What are we going to do?"

"Would you guys help me look through the things we got at Matt's apartment? Where is it all?" Georgia reached for her pack and pulled out three books, a few magazines and the plastic cylinder. "Let's put them altogether and see what we have."

Barbie and Jon emptied their packs as well and put all the contents on the couch. Georgia started with the plastic tube. She twisted the top off and carefully pulled out a roll of papers. Discarding the tube on the floor, she grabbed one end with one hand and gently stretched the papers out. Realizing that she couldn't flatten them out on the couch, she moved to the dining room table, pushing the condiments and paper napkin holder to the far side. "Give me a book," she demanded.

Barbie handed her one of the heavier books they had gathered from Matt's apartment and Georgia placed it gingerly across the top of the papers to hold them down. She used her two hands to hold the bottom tight. Now the top most one could be read, "Jin," Georgia declared. Barbie recognized the character.

Georgia went through the papers slowly. Most were small sheets, but two were folded so as to be able to fit into the tube. Barbie shook her head as she tried to figure out the significance of all this. The cheap paper was obvious to her; thick, uneven in color and texture. The expensive paper was obvious; thin, delicate, some pages almost translucent. These were the ones that Matt had signed and stamped with a square red name stamp.

"These were the practice ones," Georgia said, separating them from the rest. "The 'jin' character by itself and some whole poems. If you look, you will see that every one has the 'jin' character in it somewhere."

"What does it mean?" Barbie asked.

Georgia held up one, using her finger to retrace the characters. "This style is classic, easy to read, if you know Chinese." She looked askance at Jon who shrugged. "But this style, this swirly-whirly stuff, I have no idea. I can sort of copy it, but meaning? None of it means anything to me unless I have someone else translate it."

"And if it is Chinese poetry, it is full of metaphors and references to long dead emperors and stories of antiquity," Jon added.

"This is 'jin' for example," Georgia said, tracing a swirly-whirly character written on cheap practice paper.

"Yeah, but you never told me what 'jin' means!" Barbie whined.

Both Georgia and Jon swiveled their heads to stare at Barbie, who felt that they were in on a joke or a clue or something important and they had left her out. "I've never studied Chinese, I have no idea what it is."

"Gold," said Jon.

"It means 'gold' in Chinese. And it can also stand for money or treasure. It can be a metaphor for something precious," added Georgia.

"So, he was obsessed with this character. And the poems all had to do with the gold as well? With treasure?" Barbie asked.

"Yeah, all about gold. You remember the throwaway page stuck in the window? He did it so many times that he could afford to just throw them away." Georgia pulled out another single character 'jin'.

It was done on thin, snowy white paper. The ink was of the deepest black; the edges of the character were sharp and clear. Even Barbie could see the strength and power of the writer, the sureness of the strokes and the balance of the lines from top to bottom, left to right. And on the left, a red stamp and a tiny black notation. "His signature," Georgia explained.

"He's talented," Jon noted.

"And so ironic. He hated the Chinese, but he was good at this. He was cocky about it too. It was almost like showing up a native speaker of English by quoting Shakespeare. The other Chinese in the class used to tease him. He was a foreigner, like me, but he was so good at this. He was better at it than a number of the students who had studied for years. He never said how long he had been doing it, I suspect for years, but he never let on to the other, Chinese students. He just let them think that we had started together."

"Why did he take up Chinese calligraphy if he hated the Chinese so much? Seems like a strange hobby to me," Barbie asked.

"He had a way of quoting that saying from the Godfather," Georgia answered. "You know, 'Keep your friends close and your enemies closer.' He was going to get back at them, one of these days. I have no idea how studying calligraphy was going to help him with that."

"Do you think it would help to translate these poems?" Barbie asked. "Get a better idea of what he was thinking?"

"I don't think so. These were just copied from books and stuff. I think he was copying them for the one character, not because there was some sort of deeper meaning." Georgia looked at the stack of books and papers on the couch. "Let's divvy these up and see what we have."

Georgia stood over the couch and stared at the mess. She sighed deeply and shook her head. "What are we looking for here anyway?" She sat down at the end of the couch, next to a pile of books and caught them as they began to slide to the floor. "Anything that may tell us why Matt was in Singapore in the first place. Why was he here now? What was he doing here? He never told me that. He never really had a 'job' as such and there didn't seem to be a reason for him to be here. I'm here to be an English teacher, you guys are here to be tourists. But why was he here?"

Barbie and Jon listened carefully, but did not interrupt Georgia's monologue.

"It was something having to do with the past. He talked about the past all the time, he was truly obsessed with it. He knew his history. Of course, he knew Chinese history, all students were forced to learn it, just like we know American history, but he also knew Uyghur history, Central Asia history, and history of Tibet and Ladakh. Why? Why did he know so much about it?

"He is a minority. He is not Chinese. And, although he is a Muslim, he's not very religious, but still…" Georgia toyed with the magazines sitting next to her. They were old faded copies of National Geographic, Life Magazine, Discover Magazine with some photocopied pages of articles from other minor publications stuck in between the pages. Barbie looked and all of them were about Xinjiang, 'The land of Uyghurs,' as one proclaimed.

"He hated the Chinese." Georgia stated.

"But the calligraphy? And why the character for gold?" Barbie asked.

"Yeah, so he was a fan of history of his own people, he's interested in gold, he's anti-Chinese, so, what else do we know?" Jon asked. "And how do these people's phone numbers come into it?"

"I don't know," Georgia said, her shoulders drooping. "I don't know how they fit in. Maybe they know something? But which one? Or ones? How do they know it? And, the big one, are they telling the truth about what they know?"

By the end of this list of questions, Georgia's voice had grown shriller and she suddenly burst into tears. "Oh, I can't think, I know nothing. I'm too tired."

Barbie shoved the papers and books to the floor and reached around Georgia's shoulders. "You are too tired. You are exhausted and you need to take a hot shower, a sleeping pill and go to bed. You need some sleep. Tomorrow is another day. This can wait, we can deal with it tomorrow." She pulled Georgia to her feet and helped her towards her room.

Georgia assured Barbie that she would do as suggested and said goodnight to Barbie at the door to her room. "Goodnight and thanks for all your help. I need to calm down. Can't help anyone if I'm hysterical."

"It's serious, I know it is," Barbie assured her. "But you can't help Matt if you can't think straight. Don't worry about all this. We'll get it all sorted out and all of us can tackle it in the morning. Go to bed!"

Barbie watched as Georgia closed the door. She heard the air conditioner in her bedroom go on and knew that she was in for the night. She turned her attention to Jon and the pile on the couch. "That's your bed, you know," she said, picking up a pile and sitting next to him.

"I figured as much. It feels fine. I'm young, I can sleep anywhere. I can just take these cushions and voila." He suited actions to words and tossed the cushions from the back of the couch to the floor, making a wide firm platform. "And it's even long enough, I think."

"Georgia left me some sheets and a pillow for you, I'll go get them," she said, heading for the other bedroom.

After she had fetched the sleeping materials, she returned to the living room to find Jon playing with the small black cord that had been tied into a hangman's noose.

"Tell me you did not pick that up!" Barbie said menacingly.

"I used to do this all the time when I was a teenager, making little hangman nooses out of everything. I couldn't leave the cord there. It was as if it simply leapt into my hand as I passed by the kitchen table on the way out. It is fascinating, isn't it?"

"Fascinating, how?" the mother's voice asked.

"I had some dark times, as a teenager. So, I used to perfect my skill, making little nooses," he said simply.

"Why, why would you want to make nooses? Who did you want to hang? Oh god, you weren't suicidal, were you?" Barbie asked her eyes pleading for him to say 'no.'

"No," he laughed. "Not suicidal. Maybe patricidal, or what do you call wanting to do in your coach, coachicidal? Maybe grandpa at times was on my list. But no, just being a teenager. And it only lasted a day or two. I never said anything because by the time I talked to you on skype or the phone, the feeling was gone. But I did get good at doing this." He held up the gruesome black cord.

"I'm sorry. I never knew," Barbie gently took the cord away from Jon and put it aside. "Please tell me next time you feel like making a little hangman's noose. We can at least talk about it."

A noise startled both of them and they looked towards the master bedroom.

"Georgia," Barbie said, "I thought you had gone to bed." She shoved the cord down into the cushions. "What's the matter?"

"I need to apologize. I have been lying to you. Or rather, it was a lie by omission. Do you remember the thing I went back to get? And shoved into the side pocket of my pack?" Georgia said wearily. "Well, I have a confession to make. I took it because I thought he had forgotten it, or wasn't able to take it with him when he left. I don't know why he left it, but I knew I had to take it before someone else did. Maybe that's why I felt like we had to go back tonight. I think I knew that they were looking for this."

She held out her closed fist and slowly opened her hand. Nestled in the palm was a small, one by one by one -nch, box covered in multi-hued blue silk. A tiny silver clasp held it closed. "You see, I know that if Matt has gone somewhere, it isn't very far. And he didn't expect to be gone this long, or he was forced to go with someone. But he left behind the box, his lucky box. He has had this box since he left home, in Xinjiang, almost 20 years ago. He would never leave, move out leave, leave for good, without this box. And I had to check and make sure it was still there, the stuff inside."

"What is it? What's inside the box?" Barbie asked.

"Matt's gold. His lucky gold."

Chapter Thirteen: Looking for Gold

Barbie's eyes flew open and she came alive with excitement. "You mean, he actually had gold? His interest wasn't just fanciful or wannabe?"

Georgia laughed and opened the tiny box. Both Jon and Barbie bent forward and looked. The box was empty.

"There's nothing there," Jon pointed out.

"There is, it's just small. Tiny. Miniscule. Look," she said, turning the box upside down into her palm. A dusting of gold fell into her hand and glittered in the dim light. "Wow, I'd better put it back. There isn't really much of it. Oh look, a piece." One grain of dirt, vaguely gold colored, tumbled out of the box and came to nestle in her palm next to her heart line. "His friend gave him this gold when he left his hometown almost 20 years ago. His friend had worked in a gold mine near Hotan, in Xinjiang, and had smuggled a little bit out one day. Matt said it was a good luck charm for him, or something to remember his home by. He told me that he always took this bit of gold with him wherever he went. Whenever he moved, he took this small box. You can see that it's not much and of course not worth anything, but it was a token of friendship and always reminded him of home."

"So, his fascination with gold goes way back?" Barbie asked.

"I'm not sure if this precipitated his gold fetish, or if something else did. But it means that he didn't go far, or that he didn't plan his leaving. Do you see why I was so upset when I found the apartment ransacked? Maybe this was what they were looking for? However, the more I think of it, this is worthless except as a memento. It has no value. I'm sorry that I didn't let you know sooner, but it wasn't important as a clue. Except that I don't think Matt planned to disappear. I knew that already. I just wish he would get in touch with me, let me know what's going on."

"Let me get this straight," Jon said. "This little box, with gold dust in it, has no relationship to his writing the character 'jin' all the time? And has nothing to do with his disappearance except that he didn't take it with him? Which means that his disappearance was unplanned? Is that where we are?"

"Yeah. That's about it. I'm sorry I was so skittish this evening. I don't usually get so rattled. Right, Barbie?"

"'Cool as a cucumber Georgia' we called her. I understand. It's natural to be upset and today has been a day full of activity, surprises. And maybe something is wrong, but there is nothing else we can do today. Time for bed everyone?" Barbie looked at Jon whose eyelids had come down and at Georgia who had dark smudges under her eyes. "Things always look better in the morning light. And we will all be able to think more clearly." She smiled brightly at her two companions. "Jon looks ready to crash."

Jon's eyes were half closed and Barbie knew enough to let him sleep if he wanted. He had been a determined child, and adulthood had not changed that part of him. Georgia tipped all the gold dust she could gather and placed it back into the tiny box. She turned to her room. "Good night all. See you in the morning."

Jon mumbled something and fell back on the couch. She pushed him up and helped him make up a simple bed on the couch. As soon as the sheet was tucked in, Jon once more fell onto the couch. He grabbed a pillow and shoved it under his head.

Barbie bent and kissed him. "I haven't done that is about 15 years. You wouldn't have stood for it. But I am going to do it now. Did I tell you how happy I am that you and I are finally here, together?"

"Yeah, I guessed it. But we've never really been apart. You've always been there for me. Grandpa and Grandma Falcon were there for me physically, if I needed a rest from you-know-who and all the chaos at that house. I got to know them better because you weren't there. I think they felt obligated…"

"No, no, I told you. They never felt obligated to do anything, they loved it. You were the son they never had and you were always so precious to them. It was never a burden, never. They enjoyed every minute you spent with them."

"I know that it is so nice to have a family."

"I hope you weren't too…put out, disturbed, upset. You know, about finding out you were an 'accident?'" Barbie tentatively offered.

"Naw, time-honored tradition, that's all. Not really the way you want to start off married life, is it?"

"Not really and I hope that you are better at planning than we were."

"So far, so good," Jon grinned. "Not that I've met anyone really suited for me – yet."

"Okay, enough of this. Just like you don't really want to talk about my sex life, I don't want to know about yours. Good night, my wonderful son. I'm so happy you are here." Barbie bent and kissed him again.

Jon grunted, closed his eyes and immediately his body relaxed. Barbie touched him gently on his shoulder and turned.

"I'll just take these two books with me," she said quietly to no one. She picked up a guidebook to Xinjiang that showed a lurid orange colored desert scene on the cover. She chose another book with an equally fantastical photo of a snow-covered mountain range, a wide lake and a small contingent of horseback riders silhouetted in the foreground. She turned off the light in the living room and headed for her own bed.

A few minutes later, she slipped into the bed and nestled under the small reading light attached to the bed frame. The rest of the apartment was quiet and the hum of the air conditioner blocked out any noise from outside. It was only Barbie and her books.

She lifted the guidebook onto her knees and thumbed through. She found out immediately that 'Xinjiang' meant 'New Frontier' and that it was in far western China, more Central Asia than China. She flipped through the pages, pausing at brilliantly colored photos of deserts, mountains, colorful local Uyghurs, their donkey carts, their food, their dancing girls. Barbie had seen a photo of Matt, but had mistaken him for a Chinese. Now she studied the faces of the people in the guidebook. Some of them had brown wavy hair, round grey eyes and the men sported thick mustaches. The dancing girls had long hair in multiple braids that were topped with square hats embroidered in brilliant patterns and colors. Their dresses were of silk, multicolored and of an unusual ikat pattern. Urging herself to forgo reading details, Barbie forced herself to check the index for the city of Hotan. Her first reference was to the Hotan River and a NASA satellite photo of a vast inland desert surrounded by snow-capped mountains. The Hotan River snaked across the vast Takla Makan Desert, splitting one third of it off from the other side. Upon looking up 'Hotan' in the index, Barbie went to the pages listed. She flipped through details about the silk weaving, the origin of the dancing girls' brilliant dresses. She read of the archeologists, explorers, warlords and jade hunters. But there was no mention of gold. Disappointed, she tried the index for 'gold' and found nothing. No notations appeared, although the pages were 'browned' on the edges from being handled and read so many times. Reluctantly, Barbie put the book down. It looks like such a wonderful place, I must put this on my list of places to go.

She picked up the other book. The dust jacket was brown with age and the date on it read '1977'. The title was 'The Sinkiang Story.' Barbie thought that the S and the X were just different ways of spelling the same thing. On the fly leaf was a map of Sinkiang and Barbie found the river that cut the vast southern desert in two easily. The book was not a guide book and was arranged chronologically, so Barbie felt lost. How am I supposed to find the gold in Hotan? She flipped through pages until halfway through the book, she spied the first dogeared page. A small bend in the upper right corner caused her to stop and study the page. Then she saw it, the sentence underlined in pencil. "Reports of gold deposits near Yarkand and Khotan reinforced the desire…"

Matt was not wrong, there was gold in Hotan, and the story of being given some gold dust by a friend could certainly be true. Barbie flipped back and checked the chapter. Matt had noted this in a chapter dealing with the mid nineteenth century, a time of British and Russian push for influence in Central Asia. Barbie sighed. Almost 200 years ago, what did this have to do with Matt in Singapore in the twenty-first century? Barbie looked again and saw a dozen more notched pages.

She got up and reached for her notebook. She tried to slow her breathing and remind herself to be methodical. Write down all the pertinent information, make sure you are thorough and get it all straight. She reminded herself that being a detective like Nancy Drew was only partially adventure. A real sleuth needed details to put together, to solve the puzzle. She opened the notebook to a new page and began to write down the details. She turned to the next earmarked page. "…gold mines near Keriya, east of Khotan…" "…rich gold deposits near Yarkand and Khotan…" "…the best route from India into Kashgaria mapped in the 1860's…" "…in 1922 there were no trucks or cars in the region…" "…goods and people were transported by foot, donkey, horse and camel…" "…Sinkiang was living in the Middle Ages…" "…in 1928 gold and silver disappeared from the markets…" A section of black and white photos from the 1960's and 1970's was interleaved into the text at this point. Round Mongolian yurts alternated with herds of fluffy sheep and high two-wheeled carts drawn by horses down a street lined with trees. Her eye was sucked into one that showed a snaking line of camels in a caravan plodding up and over rippled sand dunes. It was a classic photo of exotic people in a faraway place. If this was the place that Matt was from, no wonder Georgia was fascinated in him and his stories.

Barbie turned back to the text and the dogeared pages. It was now 1944 and the revolution that had wracked China for years had come to Xinjiang. The author had lambasted the corrupt Kuomintang for their theft of wealth, stolen from the people and government of the province. He had written, "…milk the flagging economy dry." Barbie knew enough about Chinese history to begin to see where the story was leading. She flipped through pages that told of heroic efforts of a new East Turkistan Republic created by local Uyghurs, Kazakhs and other minorities to liberate their homeland from foreigners. Then she turned the page to read of the Americans, the 'quiet Americans' who thought they were 'defending the free world and the values of Western civilization' by colluding with corrupt Kuomintang officials in the capital Urumqi. The page with this story was heavily underlined, as if the reader needed to sear the treachery into his consciousness.

A few pages later was another heavily underlined earmarked page that told the story of three corrupt Kuomintang officials in Urumqi who conspired to sell the government goods in their possession. They sold the equipment to a local representative of the People's Liberation Army, and "…with a small bodyguard made off for the Indian border…" Another set of miscreants had gone over the Karakoram Pass, according to the book, and presumably these three did as well.

What caused Barbie to look again was the note about the amount of gold they had received. "They got their price of eight hundred 'lan' of gold…" An asterisk after the word 'lan' alerted her to the bottom of the page and the footnote. "One lan equals one and one-third ounces." The light above Barbie's head was dim, but she could just make out a faint set of figures that had been erased. She ran her fingers over the page and could feel the faint marks left behind. She took her own pencil and traced over them. 800 x 1.33. And then the neat columns that added up to 1064 oz. Then the notes of 66.5 lb. and then 30.22kg.

"Thirty kilos of gold," she said out loud. She remembered that Georgia had said that Matt had rattled on about 30 kilos of gold and Barbie immediately thought that she had been mistaken in her interpretation, that somehow it was a metaphor for betrayal and really was 30 pieces of gold, or rather silver. But no, Matt had not been referring to 30 pieces of gold or silver, but in fact to 30 kilos of gold. Stolen in September 1949.

Chapter Fourteen: Fast Food Breakfast

Barbie flipped backwards and forwards in the book, looking for more references. Finally, she turned to the index and in desperation, the internet on her phone. There was nothing. No mention, ever again, of the three culprits who had 'made off for the Indian border.' What happened to them? Did they make it to India? With all their loot? And their bodyguard? What happened to them? Were they paid off with the ill-gotten gains? How many were there? In September? Was that a good time of year? And after India, where did they go from there? The only 'safe' place was Taiwan, the redoubt of the Kuomintang, and the home of Chiang Kai-Shek. Maybe Hong Kong, a cauldron of activity, full of foreigners and upheavals?

Barbie thought of what she knew about the world in 1949. In America, it was four years after the end of the War. It was the year her father was born. It was a country at peace, heading for growth and prosperity.

But what of the rest of the world? Especially Asia? Civil war, famines, new countries, new alliances. And people on the move. It would have been easy to 'lose' themselves among the teeming masses seeking new homes and shifting political alliances. What was the price of gold in 1949? How far could they go on 30 kilos? The questions would not stop.

Exhausted, she slipped a piece of paper into the book at the exciting page and put it on the bedside table. She slipped out from under the sheet and went to the door. Cautiously she opened the door and peeked into the darkened living room. She had hoped Jon would still be awake, but the sounds of soft snoring greeted her. She tiptoed across the room using the ambient light from her bedside lamp to approach Georgia's bedroom door. There was no light coming from under the door. Barbie pressed her ear against the door and strained to hear anything.

"All quiet on the front," she murmured to herself and then softly made her way back to bed. She got into bed and picked up the book again. Less than a minute later, she put it down and turned out the light. Exhaustion swept over her like a gigantic wave, carrying her off to slumber land.

The noises that crept into her brain were aided by the sunlight streaming through the window to jerk her into wakefulness. Sleep stuck in her eyes and she carefully wiped it away, wiping the cobwebs with it. Then she smelled the coffee. A quick look at her watch and she knew it was time to be up. She knew Georgia's routine, up early and jog around the neighborhood. She thought, given the hour, that Georgia may have been up for hours. She threw on her clothes and emerged into the room that functioned as a living and dining room. She found Georgia and Jon drinking coffee. Georgia wore running clothes and sported a sheen of sweat on her face. Jon looked like he had recently emerged from a winter's bear den. His hair stuck up and stubble scarred his face.

"I see you've been running already?" Barbie queried Georgia.

"Yes, and I hope you have had a good night's sleep, ready for another day?" Georgia said brightly.

"Yes, a good night. And I was reading until late, and wait until you hear what I found," Barbie said enthusiastically.

"Good," Georgia said, rising from her seat. "I'll shower, and then we can go find some breakfast and you can tell us all about it!" She pushed away from the table and was off to her bedroom.

Barbie's mouth hung open. She felt brushed aside, but on second thought, she shrugged and got herself a cup of coffee. She turned to Jon. "Good morning. How did you sleep?"

"Great. I'm not used to the air conditioning and I got too cold in the night. I just woke up myself. How are you today?" Jon yawned and slurped his coffee.

"I'm good. Late night, reading until all hours. I guess I'll have to wait until Georgia's ready to hear all this." Barbie fiddled with her coffee cup. "So, what do you want to do today? Do you want to continue helping us figure out where Matt has gone, or would you prefer to take a boat ride on the river, visit museums…? What?"

"Let's see what Georgia has in mind. I'm easy." Jon finger combed his wild mop of hair, in hue and curliness, very much like his mother's.

Barbie chortled with amusement. "You still do that? The finger comb, rather than a comb or brush? Do you even have a comb?"

Jon laughed with her. "Of course, I have a comb, but I'm not sure where it is. If it gets too much, I just have it cut."

They reminisced a few minutes longer and then Georgia appeared. "Ready?" she trilled.

"Not yet, but soon." Barbie announced.

Within ten minutes they were out the door and standing in front of the food court, which was situated on the ground floor of the building next door. Barbie counted seven small counters, of which only three appeared to be open. Pictures of the food served at each one was displayed above the counter, along with the price. One sported a green star and crescent, which Barbie took to mean a Muslim restaurant, serving halal food. Georgia headed straight for one that had a short line. Barbie and Jon followed.

"Soy milk and cakes? A great breakfast," Georgia said. "I'll order. If you want, you can go and get some more coffee. I'd like a cup of coffee with milk. It's condensed milk, so you don't need any extra sugar. Otherwise, black is REALLY black."

Jon and Barbie headed for the Coffee Shop which also had a short line. Barbie watched the aproned cook behind the counter. Do they call them baristas here? It surely is specialized. Barbie watched with fascination as the man took a huge metal pitcher with a long spout and began to slowly pour black steaming liquid into another identical pitcher. As he poured, he stretched the 'pour' to the limit of his arms, sending an aromatic stream of coffee from one to the other. He slowly shortened the pour as he finished, and then switched pitchers, pouring the coffee back into the first pitcher. In the back, Barbie watched another 'barista' preparing two more coffee jugs. He grabbed a darkly stained cheesecloth 'sock' from a row above his head and ladled freshly ground coffee into it until it hung heavy in his hand. He lowered it into one pitcher, carefully tightening it around the rim, and then prepared a similar sock for the second pitcher. A strong acrid smell of coffee hung over the establishment. Barbie inched over, leaving the ordering and buying to Jon, as she watched steaming water flow out of a special tap in the wall into the newly prepared pitcher.

"Mom," hissed Jon. "Do you have any money? I forgot mine."

Barbie shook her head. Kids, never have money. She reached for her wallet. As she looked down at the three cups of coffee on the small tray in front of her, she could see dark brown liquid with a sheen of oil floating on top. "Where's the milk?" she asked Jon.

"It's in there, believe me. I saw them do it. Straight from the condensed milk can. But you are right in thinking it doesn't look like it. Coffee strong enough to put hair on your chest, like it or not!" Jon laughed as he carried the tray to the table where Georgia waited for them.

The table had been wiped clean, if still slightly sticky, but Barbie shrugged it off. This was Singapore and she felt sure that it was clean enough. Jon had toughened his stomach to tolerate more germs than this table had, and she had been living in Turkey and Egypt for a couple of years. Singapore germs had nothing on what they had endured. Georgia had bought a selection of yellow cakes and long fried doughnut sticks, ridged and dusted with powdered sugar. With the coffee and hot soy milk, they had a feast.

The soy milk was unlike any that Barbie had ever tasted, slightly sweet and with the undertones of something burnt. The color was also slightly off. But it was satisfying.

After a few bites to stave off starvation, Barbie could hold her story no longer. "I found it, I found the 30 kilos of gold."

"Good heavens. Where? When?" Georgia asked. "I assume that you mean you have found the reason why Matt talked about it."

"Yes, in the 'Sinkiang Story' book. I was just looking, and I found notes and underlinings. And listen to this." She pulled the book out of her bag and opened it to the page marked by Matt.

"That's the one that he read to me from. History from the invaders' point of view, he called it. He would read and then laugh and give me his version of the story." Georgia took the book from Barbie and looked hard at it, flipping through some pages.

"Have you read it?" Barbie asked.

"No, he never offered to let me read it, although it's in English, unlike a lot of his books. But he talked about it."

"Listen to this," Barbie commanded, taking the book back from Georgia and reading the three paragraphs aloud. As she finished "…and over the Karakoram Pass," Georgia took the book and looked at it again.

"Coffee one more?" asked a young man who had unexpectedly materialized at the table. He had a tray and was collecting empty plates and coffee cups.

"Yes, please," Georgia answered. "Three cups of coffee, can or not?"

"Can, can!" came the answer, as the young waiter scurried away.

"Is that Singlish?" Barbie asked.

"Yes, and I am often not sure what I've said. But I think we will get three cups of coffee, not three for each of us." Georgia turned her attention back to the book.

As Georgia read, flipping pages, Jon and Barbie turned to watch the neighbors. High rise apartments loomed all around them. The grounds were interspersed with green grass, trees with umbrella-like foliage and crisscrossed with covered walkways. The ground floors of most buildings had small shops, food courts or were totally empty. It did not seem crowded, not like Chinatown crowded, but the density of the population was discernible.

"Thirty kilos of gold," Georgia said aloud. "I am trying to remember what he said about it. Where did this come from and where did it lead? I'm sure this is what he was talking about. This is it. The story is in one of his favorite books, it is underlined, he did the math here. Yes, this is it. But where did the gold go? No answers here. Nothing else, that I can find. And he had read this book, all of it, so if there was something else, he would have found it, he would have marked it, underlined it, noted it. Somehow, he would have linked this up. But we are missing some pieces of the puzzle. Here, this is Kashgar," she opened the end leaf of the book and pointed to the city marked 'Kashgar' on the map. "This area is Kashgaria." Her fingered twirled in a circle that included the westernmost part of the map. "Here is Hotan, Matt's hometown. And here," she traced a route from Hotan with her finger to a break in the border line, "is the Karakoram Pass. And Kashmir, which is India. The three Kuomintang traitors would have to go this way."

"They had to go through Matt's hometown. Three Chinese with a bodyguard..." Jon said.

"With 30 kilos of gold," Barbie finished his sentence. "Not easy to hide."

"But this was all years and years ago. What does it have to do with today?" Georgia said too loudly.

The young waiter appeared again, very stealthily, and placed three cups of coffee on the table. Georgia absentmindedly gave him a bill, which caused him to beam happily and he rushed to take away their empties. Barbie looked at the deep black liquid and felt her stomach churn with distaste. Maybe I won't have any more of this powerful stuff. She toyed with it as she listened to Georgia.

"What if,' Georgia started. "I'm just thinking here. What if the 30 kilos of gold never made it to India. What if…"

Barbie grabbed the book and flipped to the dog-eared page. She read again, "…made off for the Indian border." It doesn't say, 'arrived safely in…' or even 'arrived in.' Just "made off for…"

"Thirty kilos of gold."

Chapter Fifteen: Jon Makes a Visit

Jon interrupted Georgia's reverie to ask for Yannis' phone number. He took out his phone with the new Singapore SIM card and tried it. "Working, just like they promised it would. Great, I now feel free!" He punched in the number as Barbie read it off from her notebook. As the number rang, he stood up from the table and walked off a distance. They could hear the first part of his conversation. "Hello, Yannis, this is Jon. We met yesterday…"

Georgia and Barbie sat and stared at the book as it lay on the table between them. "What else might there be in this book?" Barbie asked. "Should we read all of it?"

"Dunno. We need to go through it thoroughly, but I suspect you have seen the best of it, with the dog-eared and underlined pages. I need to remember what he told me."

Jon walked back to the table. "All set, I'm meeting him in an hour at the dojo. Georgia, maybe you can help me. Here's the address," he said, pulling out a small notebook and referring to a page with tiny handwriting.

Georgia looked at the notebook and said, "Do you, both of you, always carry a notebook?"

Jon and Barbie looked at each other. Jon raised his eyebrows and Barbie giggled. "Detectives always have a notebook to write things down. We've always been 'detectives'," Barbie answered. "I started on Nancy Drew as a child, and he started on Agatha Christie at age 10 or 11."

"Dashiell Hammed, Raymond Chandler, all the Charlie Chan novels," Jon added. "Just a hobby." He looked guiltily at Georgia. "Nothing like this."

"You two are having fun, aren't you? My Matt is missing, maybe..." Georgia choked and stopped. "And you guys are playing detectives."

"No," they answered together.

"We know this is real," Barbie continued. "It's just that some of this is so much like a novel. All mysteries are, to an extent. Never mind our notebooks, let's get to work."

"How do I get to the dojo?" Jon asked.

Georgia asked for the address and then checked it on her phone. "Not far from Chinatown. This is how you get there..."

They went back to Georgia's apartment and looked at the dining room table, now covered with the books, magazines, photocopies and notes from Matt's apartment.

"The answer's here, I know it is," Georgia said.

"Let's do it this way. Each of us sits down, equidistant from each other, and starts on the book or paper nearest us. If we find anything, anything that is at all relevant, we put it aside for a second read." Barbie organized them.

"I'm leaving soon," Jon said, "so let me start with this small stack here," he said, sitting down in front of a thin pile of magazines.

"Right you are," Georgia conceded. She sat in front of a stack of notebooks and photocopied papers.

Barbie took a seat and looked at the three books in front of her. She added the book that she had found so useful to the stack. Then she picked up another book and started on it. She checked the table of contents, the index, and flipped through the pages. None were earmarked nor did there appear to be any underlined passages. She surreptitiously checked on the other two, who were doggedly, if unsuccessfully, doing the same.

Soon Jon stood. "I'm off now. I'll call when I'm finished. Should I come back here?"

"Yeah, why not? We'll be here." Georgia went back to her browsing.

After Jon had departed, Barbie stopped looking and turned to Georgia. "Why calligraphy? Why did Matt want to do calligraphy? You said yourself that he hated Chinese, so why would he want to write in the language?"

"I've asked myself that, at least since Matt disappeared. I never really questioned him when he was here, when we were doing it. I guess I was interested in the art and I just assumed he was as well. I know that he was fluent in Chinese, but that his tones weren't great. I don't know if he really spoke it well. The calligraphy was, I think, like me, done as a hobby. Just playing around with the brush and ink."

"What kinds of things did he write?" Barbie asked.

"Old poems. Anything with 'jin' in it. In fact, that's what prompted him to tell me about the gold dust in the box. I thought it was sentimental only, you know, thoughts of the old homestead. But then he mentioned the 30 kilos of gold."

"Okay," Barbie asked, "what exactly did he say? Exactly."

Georgia closed her eyes and scrunched up her face. Her body was completely still. Barbie waited. Then she began to count the seconds. Finally, after more than one minute, Georgia opened her eyes and heaved a mighty sigh. "Here goes, to the best of my recollection."

Barbie reached for her notebook and prepared to take notes.

"I do NOT remember the context. I don't know what we'd been talking about or doing. We were here, as a matter of fact, in my living room, sitting at this table. He had his gold box with him, I don't know why. I had heard the story of 'the gold and his friend from his hometown' already. He got a bit dreamy, reminiscing dreamy. He said, '…stories of lost treasure. My grandfather told me stories of caravans lost in the desert, going through the mountains, laden with treasure. Lost in the sands, lost in the snow.' That, of course, could refer to anything, anytime. Then he said, 'My grandfather mentioned one treasure he saw himself. We didn't believe him. It was too fantastic. But maybe he was right.' Then he stopped talking. A few minutes later he said, 'But I think I've found it; 30 kilos of gold.' I asked him what it meant and he said, 'Nothing.' He never said anything else about it. He talked like that a lot. I never wanted to pressure him.

"He had an incredible life. He had traveled all over China, he studied in Beijing, traveled to Shanghai. I think he had even been to Russia. He came to Singapore from Malaysia. And like I said, I am not sure if he was even legal here in Singapore. I just have this feeling that if I can find out why he left, I could find out where he is."

"Makes sense to me, but where do we start? Oh," Barbie said quietly to herself. "We have started."

Georgia's phone rang just then, a small tinkling sound from the bedroom. She got up to answer it. At first Barbie heard only a soft voice answering and greeting someone. Then Georgia's voice rang out.

"Not fair. It is NOT my job. I did all the…" Georgia lowered her tone and continued to talk. Barbie tried to concentrate on the books in front of her.

"I have to go to work," Georgia stormed back into the room. "Someone… Never mind. I have to go to the office for a few hours, not many, I hope."

"I'm sorry," Barbie commiserated. "What happened?"

"Oh, one of my colleagues 'did a Changi'. I have been requested, or ordered, to come and clean up the mess. Student files, grades etc.," she answered.

"'Did a Changi'? Is that another Singlish expression?" Barbie asked.

"No, it's foreigner-speak for 'up and leaving.' If you just get fed up or your employer fires you or has a dispute and cancels your visa, you just go to Changi airport and take the next flight out. 'Doing a Changi' happens all the time with foreigners. The culture is different, even if it looks like a Western culture, and the work ethic is radically different, all skewed in favor of the employer. Us Westerners sometimes have trouble dealing with it. Hence the abrupt leaving.

Anyway, I have to go. I'll be back soon. I'll call you when I'm done. You have a key. There is food in the fridge."

"I'll just stay here, wait for Jon. And I'll keep working on these books and papers."

"You are a star!" Georgia said as she disappeared into her bedroom to get her things.

The door slammed behind Georgia and Barbie was all alone with the dining room table and the piles of papers. For a few minutes she sat and shuffled through them, trying to find a pattern. Why had Georgia selected these? What did she hope to find in this collection that was important? Why not take all of them? Well, dummy, there were hundreds of books and magazines and a couple of boxes full of papers. We couldn't take all of them. Which brings us back to, why these? Barbie suddenly felt tired, as if she had not had a good nights' sleep, which she hadn't. I'll just take this one and go lie down for a while.

She picked up the guidebook to Xinjiang, the one with colorful pictures of the exotic places and slipped into her room. She gently closed the door, trying to close off the rest of the unsorted material. She made herself comfortable on the bed and opened the guidebook. At first, she flipped through pages, looking at the sumptuous photographs and reading sidebars and short pieces, not trying to absorb anything thoroughly. Then she backtracked to the beginning. She began to piece together a story about the Silk Road that had made Xinjiang a pivotal character in the road between China and Europe. The oases along the desert routes were vital to the maintenance of the many 'Silk Roads' and Hotan was once a very grand place. She leaned back and tried to absorb this information.

Visions of camel trains, plodding over desert sand dunes, reawakened her memories of camel trekking in Egypt. The sway and creak of the wooden saddles, the sound of whispering wind over the sand gullies, the soft murmur of the camel men who walked while the foreigners rode. She smiled at the memory of the camel who had reached her head around and untied Barbie's shoe lace. Something about Barbie jerking on the reins to stop her mount from exploring the delicious looking weeds by the side of the trail, and control of the speed and direction of travel, Barbie couldn't remember the whole scenario, but the memory was pleasant. Then she drifted to visions of what it would be like in present day Xinjiang. Would the camels be the two-humped Bactrian variety that she had seen in the photos? Are they different in gait and feel from the one-humped kind in the Middle East? She imagined herself on a camel, a soft blanket laid in between the humps, the gentle sway in time to music.

That was what was missing, music. She reached for her phone and punched in, 'Uyghur music'. She saw a YouTube video of a dancing girl and clicked on it. Soon the phone was playing the soft swaying sounds of singing girls, long-necked instruments and drums. Barbie picked up the book again and found photos of weddings, musical performances and imagined the taste of long green grapes, freshly baked bread and plates of spicy kebabs. She closed her eyes and leaned back on the pillows. The camel undulated under her, and the music played with the sway of the beast. The music moved faster and the camel started to go faster to keep up.

Barbie felt the rapid movements and grabbed to hang on, the drums beats came faster and then louder and louder. The camel leaped forward and bounced down hard, causing Barbie to reach for the reins, the pommel. There were none. The camel jumped forward again and Barbie felt as though she was going to slip off. The pounding drums beat louder and louder, the camel began to run faster and faster. Barbie felt herself slipping and cried out as she flew off. She hit the ground and a loud panicked scream emerged from her throat. From the ground, she looked up, but the camel blanket obscured her view, she tried to fling it off, but it acted as a noose, coming down to cover her entire head, cutting off air.

"Georgia, Mom, is anyone there??" The banging come through the muffled bedclothes over her head. Barbie shook her head and threw off the sheet that had entangled itself over her head.

"Jon," she called. "Jon? Is that you?"

"Mom? Open the door, will you? I don't have a key!" Jon's voice came loudly and clearly from the front door to the apartment. "And I NEED to talk to you. Now."

Chapter Sixteen: Dim Sum Lunch

"Georgia, I'm so glad you came back! Jon has news. He's been to the dojo and he has something to tell us!" Barbie said, in greeting to Georgia as she walked in the door.

"Well, not a lot, but adding to the knowledge," Jon replied. "I know where we can find Bruce Lee tonight. Unless you want to call him yourself, you have the phone number."

"Hmmm. Let me think on that. My business is finished. They have agreed to pay me extra, so I am satisfied, at least not as angry as I was. Anybody hungry?" Georgia said, sitting down with a plop on the couch.

"Do you want to know what I learned?" Jon asked, slightly hurt by Georgia's attitude.

Barbie noticed Jon's distress. "Yeah, we'll get all the details as soon as we have some food in our stomachs. I could certainly eat. What about you, Jon? Hungry?"

"We can have dim sum. It's nearby," said Georgia. "Yes, Jon, I am interested, but my stomach comes first. It's a thing with me, sorry. Are we ready to go? It's not far." Georgia then began to prepare for the next outing.

Within fifteen minutes they were seated at a round table in yet another food court. They had ordered from a menu, indicating how many of what kind of small bites of food. Almost immediately, a series of small plates appeared, each containing two or three small steamed buns, rolls, and dumplings, each with a different filling. Small dishes of soy sauce, vinegar, and chile were also placed on the table. Three sets of chopsticks were slammed down on the table by a harried waitress.

After a few quick bites, Georgia sighed and turned to Jon. "Tell me what you found out in the dojo."

Jon swallowed a bite of dumpling, while juices ran down his chin. No napkins meant he used the back of his hand to wipe his face. "First, about Yannis. I think I found out why he didn't want to be seen by the surveillance cameras yesterday, at least why he kept out of sight of the one in the park. He's overstayed his visa. He came in legally, but has stayed to work. When he leaves, he's likely to be stuck with a fine. He's done nothing illegal, except work and overstay his visa, so he probably wouldn't be put in jail. Unless they found out he was working illegally, then it may be more difficult. He's paid in cash, and most of it directly by his students at the dojo. He's a teacher. So when he leaves, he will not be able to come back. So, make hay while the sun shines, as they say. At the moment he feels safe, but doesn't want anyone to 'out' him to the police. Frankly, he would rather not be seen at all. He says he often grows a beard or mustache and then shaves it off, wears different hats almost everywhere. He has a collection. He wears dull, ordinary clothes and tries not to attract notice by his height. He didn't really say much about his odd behavior yesterday, but now we know why. He volunteered this information to me, by the way."

"I wonder if it is true," Georgia said. "I feel I can trust him, but I'm not always the best judge of character."

"Now, Bruce Lee," Jon continued, expertly grabbing another dumpling and shoving it into his mouth. As he bit into it, a squirt of aromatic ginger-flavored sauce flew across the table. "Sorry," he mumbled.

"Don't talk with your mouth full," said Barbie in a scolding mother's voice, then chuckled at herself.

Jon chewed, swallowed and then continued. "I found out the source of at least some of Matt's money. He was involved in the trade in fake aphrodisiacs. So is Yannis, but not to the extent that Matt was. Matt contacted his 'people' in Malaysia. Did he go to Malaysia often?" Jon asked Georgia.

"Yes, he said he had friends there and he came in through Malaysia, that I do know. And he might have a Malaysian passport as well," Georgia added. "So he was importing these drugs, fake Viagra let's call it, through Malaysia?"

"That's it. The route is from China, through Thailand and then Malaysia. When it gets here, Matt helps Bruce Lee distribute it in the red-light districts in Singapore." Jon continued.

"Wait a minute," said Barbie. "Yannis is involved in this as well?"

"Yeah," Jon said.

"So," Barbie intoned. "Yannis has overstayed his visa, is working illegally as a martial arts teacher in a dodgy dojo, and he helps smuggle, distribute and sell fake drugs. No wonder he wants to hide out from the authorities."

"Put that way, he does sound shifty," Georgia said. "But he's a nice guy," she added.

"A businessman." Jon said helpfully. "Anyway, Yannis thinks that Matt has disappeared, voluntarily, because of aggressive turf battles about the fake Viagra. He thinks Matt has gone underground."

"In Singapore? Or somewhere else?" Georgia asked.

"He's not sure. But he did tell me where to find Bruce Lee tonight. Bruce should know more. We can ask him. I've got the street corner written down where he works. It's in Geylang, in the red-light district." Jon smiled and showed them the penciled address.

"We? You want to take your mother to a red-light district?" Barbie almost shouted.

"You'd be with me, it's safe. There are police around everywhere. Prostitution is legal in Singapore because they figure they can't squash it. The 'world's oldest profession' and all that. And it's highly regulated. Don't worry, I'll be safe from the girls because I'll be with women and you will be safe with me. We're just tourists."

"Hmmm," Georgia said.

"Well, you have Bruce Lee's phone number, we could just call him?" Jon prompted Georgia.

"No, I've thought about that. I don't want to call anyone in that phone list. I don't want anyone to know that I have found Matt's phone. If he has gone underground, then it's best to keep it hidden." Georgia stared into space, thinking.

Barbie grabbed another pork bun and nibbled on it. It was too big to put in her mouth in one bite, but hard to hold onto with chopsticks. Finally, she took it in one hand and ate it. The red pork filling oozed out and she licked it up. She thought that she and Jon hadn't gotten the feel of this stuff yet; Georgia seemed to be doing better.

Georgia's phone rang. She pulled it out of her bag and looked at the number. "Funny, no number," she mumbled. "Hello," she said into the phone. Barbie looked at her and watched as her eyes lit up and a wide smile split her face. "Matt," she said.

Barbie and Jon held their breath, trying to be as quiet as possible so that Georgia could carry on a conversation. They, too, smiled broadly as this unexpected phone call.

"Where are you?" Georgia demanded. "Okay, okay, I'm listening. Haw Par Villa, yes. 'Jin', gotcha. Where are you? When are you coming back? You'll call later? Okay, wait, Matt, wait. Matt, Matt!"

Georgia reluctantly lowered the now buzzing phone. At first her face registered puzzlement, then she heaved a tremendous sigh of relief. "At least he called. At least he's alive. At least I know."

"But, where is he?" Barbie demanded.

"He didn't say, exactly. But he did say 'Haw Par Villa. Go to Haw Par Villa.' And 'look for the 'jin', the sign of the 'jin'. Then he hung up." Georgia looked puzzled and relieved alternatively.

"What is the 'Haw Par Villa'?" Barbie asked.

"The Tiger Balm Gardens. They are Chinese gardens, I've been there. And he said look for the sign of 'jin'. I'm sure there is something there like that. All the signs are in Chinese and English. We just have to find the right one. I've been there, he took me, so I can go back to places we saw. I'm sure he would tell me to go somewhere that he has taken me. All we have to do is find the 'jin'." Her face then showed dismay. "But the place is huge! And there are lots of signs. Lots of 'jin'."

"You must know something more than just going to a huge garden with signs and look for one character in a Chinese sign? How will you know when you get there? And then, what will you find?" Barbie felt cheated at the phone call.

"Oh, I'm not really worried, he'll call me back."

"What are we looking for?" Jon asked. "When we find the sign, then what? Can you call him back?"

Georgia went back to her phone and tried to find the phone number that had called her. "There is no number and no way to return the call. Out of luck, I guess. But I'm not going to worry," she said confidently. "Matt and I had a system. Remember that I told you we had a deal that we would call each other almost every day. It was just checking in with each other, but he had a method of keeping in touch. That's why I was so worried about him. He didn't call. Now I know he's alright. And I know he'll call again. I know."

"But he didn't say much, did he?" Barbie asked.

"No, but he said enough. I know."

"What are you looking for? At the 'jin' sign?" Barbie persisted.

"Well, the connection wasn't very good, so there were some parts of the message I didn't get too well. But I did get the Tiger Balm Gardens part and the 'jin' part," Georgia said.

"Does it have to do with his work? The smuggling of the drugs?" Jon persisted. "Now that Yannis has told me about the fake Viagra, was that what this was all about?"

"Maybe," Georgia answered. "I just know that he called and asked. It's a public place for heaven's sake. It's daylight. What could happen? He'll call me again when we get there.

He'll wait until we are there and then he will call. It's our way. Our 'modus operandi'. We used to phone, and discuss where to meet, and never say exactly where. When we got in the vicinity, we would phone again until we met each other. I know it sounds convoluted, but Matt was into this secrecy thing. He loved playing cat and mouse and chase. It was a game."

"I hope this is just another game," Barbie said. "We'll go with you and do our Singapore sightseeing. Support you, because you are our friend. I hope you find what you are supposed to find."

"Don't worry, he'll call. I'm not worried," Georgia said. "I'm not worried, we will find it."

"What is it that we'll find? What are we looking for?" Barbie said again.

"Drugs… or gold?" Jon asked.

Chapter Seventeen: The Haw Par Villa

Barbie insisted, "I'll pay. We are guests and we will pay something. We cannot fall back totally on your goodwill."

"But you are giving up your vacation to help me," Georgia insisted back.

"I, for one, have seen more of the most interesting parts of Singapore than I could ever have imagined. Onwards to the Gardens," Jon rejoined.

Once more on public transport, Barbie realized that the Haw Par Villa had its own MRT station and that it was not far away. It was midafternoon before they arrived. Few people were on the train and as it was the end of the line, few passengers got off. They walked through a spacious, new station and when they walked outside, the bright sun hit them. Jon sneezed and reached for his sunglasses. Barbie shoved a hat on her head and Georgia pulled out a long-sleeved cotton shirt from her bag. Directly in front of them was a huge empty parking lot bordered by tall trees, and beyond that, the entrance to the old-fashioned amusement park.

A wide road led up from the park, but only pedestrians used it now. Massive gates stood open and a kiosk off to the left gave out information rather than taking in money. A lone official-looking uniformed man sat in the booth. A large sign next to the kiosk indicated that entrance was free.

"What is this place anyway?" asked Jon.

"You know about Tiger Balm, don't you? The cure-all Chinese medicine? One of the three brothers, children of the inventor, built this place. There is a villa at the top of the hill, much changed unfortunately, with a grand view of the ocean. The rest of the gardens are filled with edifying tableaux from Chinese folk tales. The idea was to get the Chinese of Singapore to come here, learn their history and folk tales and leave morally uplifted. You'll see. There used to be more of a 'fun fair' atmosphere, with boat rides and shows in the small amphitheater, but it has fallen on hard times. The city of Singapore has taken it over and it's being renovated, slowly. But still an amusing sight to see."

They walked through the gates and up the hill. Barbie noted the crumbling statues, peeling paint, dying potted plants and moldy rivulets of water leaking from rusty pipes. Then they came to the first of the tableaux and she became enchanted. The figures were still crumbling, many lacked limbs, their headdresses were cracked and the ground littered with leaves and debris. But the scene was of a battle between mice and rabbits, with a lavishly dressed Oriental god overseeing it all. Splashes of red paint covered the hillsides and the raised swords. She looked again, and saw that some of the missing limbs were meant to be missing, cut off by the victorious Mice. It was a gruesome scene and Barbie began to understand what Georgia had said about the efforts to teach and 'edify' the population. Was this a battle between good and evil?

"Barbie, come on!" Georgia said from her right. "This way. I think I want to check out the Ten Courts of Hell first. I think it is the most likely place to find a 'jin' sign. Besides, it was one of the places Matt took me, so it stands to reason that it might be a place where he would assume I might go. This way."

Georgia led the way, past a pagoda that 'floated' in a pond, a tea house, now closed, and the way to the amphitheater.

"What are we looking for?" Jon asked.

"A sign that says 'jin'. You know the character, even Barbie does." Georgia answered, a trifle irritated.

"I know that," Jon answered. "I just want to know what is at this sign. The sign itself is only that, a sign. A sign of what?"

A gardener passed behind Barbie as she hurried to stay up with Georgia and Jon. He was a small man, dressed in a loose-fitting pair of coveralls, pushing an empty wheelbarrow. Barbie stopped to look at him. Then she became distracted by the figures in a small niche. Suddenly she found herself alone. She stopped and looked all around. Jon, Georgia and the gardener were gone, she was by herself. A large hedge blocked her way forward. Then she heard voices.

"Jon, Georgia," Barbie called out. "Are you there?"

A younger man, dressed in a guard uniform, stepped out of the hedge. "Mam," he said, "please not shout here."

"I've lost my friends, sorry. Have you seen them?" she asked, a hint of panic creeping into her voice.

"They had gone this way. Please, no shout, this not playground," he answered. He pointed to the hedge, which Barbie realized was not solid. She smiled brightly and passed through the opening. She saw the two not far from her, standing in front of a large long low building. She scurried towards them.

Georgia was explaining, exasperated. "We'll find out when we get there. He'll call. Here we are," she announced as they approached the elaborate gate. A notice stood at the entrance.

Barbie read, "Ten Courts of Hell. The 'Ten Courts of Hell' is dedicated to the teaching of traditional values through Chinese folklore. Due to the graphics nature of the exhibits, viewers' discretion and prarental guidance are advised." She snickered, "Georgia, they need you here. Look at this sign." She pointed to the misspelling and the grammatical mistake.

They entered and immediately, Jon removed his dark glasses. Lurid colored lights dimly lit ten tableaux, the ten courts of hell. Georgia walked quickly from one to the other, starting with the First Court. Barbie understood immediately why the viewers' discretion was advised. Punishments consisted of disembowelment, ripping out hearts and cutting off limbs. Signs on each court identified the crimes and the punishments, graphically illustrated by one-third life-size figurines. Robed enforcers armed with swords and knives stood over naked figures with missing arms and legs and bloody chests. Red paint was dispersed on every surface.

Barbie quickly passed by the first few, glancing at the signs, which were in two languages, as promised. She saw nothing at first pass that said 'gold' and then she remembered that 'jin' could also mean other things. She went back and joined Georgia and Jon as they scrutinized one sign in particular.

"Here's one for teachers," he joked. "Cheating during examinations," he read, "intestines and organs pulled out." As expected, the small figures illustrated the gruesome penalty for cheaters. The grimacing faces of the hapless victims reflected the pain and suffering as their innards were pulled from their bellies. The intestines, dripping blood and spilling over the errant students' bodies, were meant to emphasize and thoroughly frighten the children of Singapore so they would never, ever try cheating.

Fascinated, Barbie involuntarily shuddered. "A friend told me that her German grandmother told her a frightening story about a gremlin or a ghost that would come in the night and snatch and eat her tongue if she continued to suck her thumb. It frightened her so much that she never sucked her thumb again. So, this kind of thing works, but I wonder about the psychological damage done."

"Buck teeth all your life or a little psychological damage??" Georgia asked.

Barbie twisted her face into a disapproving grimace. "Never had a kid," she whispered to Jon.

Jon shrugged, "Never sucked my thumb and never had to cheat, so I don't have an opinion."

"Here," Georgia said. "Look, a 'jin' sign." She stood before the Fifth Court where a sign said that moneylenders would be thrown on a hill of knives.

Jon and Barbie caught up with her and stared at the lurid treatment of moneylenders. A hillside, covered with the blades of knives sticking up out of the soil like pointed rocks, had several statues, writhing and covered in their own blood. The knives protruded all the way through their naked bodies, as if a giant had thrown them down violently.

"Here is the 'gold' sign." Georgia pointed to the sign that contained a small character within many others. She looked at the scene and then looked around. They had seen no other patrons and the park workers were about their business.

Before she could be stopped, Georgia leapt gracefully over the short cement wall and entered the tableaux. The red and yellow lights glowed eerily on her skin. She first approached the sign and looked behind it. "It's dark back here, but it's not a large space any way. Maybe farther back."

"Why don't you use the light on your phone?" Barbie suggested.

"What are you looking for?" Jon asked. "I could help if I knew what it was. Bigger than a bread box?"

Georgia shrugged. "I don't know what I'm looking for. And yeah, the light on the phone would be good." She crept further into the exhibit and turned on the phone's light, which glowed faintly. "Whoa, I need to turn this off. My battery is low. I need to save it for when Matt calls." She came back to the front of the exhibit and stepped over the wall. "And besides, you're right, I don't know what I'm looking for. It looks like a sad little, old-fashioned fun park. Who would hide or put anything here?"

"Maybe because it is, small, sad and old-fashioned. No one's here, quiet. No one would suspect a shipment of drugs, would they?" Barbie said. "Is that what you are looking for Georgia?"

"Ummmm," Georgia answered. "Let's see if there are any more 'jin' signs?"

She started to quickly walk through the other Courts of Hell, followed by Barbie and Jon. They all looked, reading every sign, trying to decide if a 'jin' might be in the translation. They found no more references to gold or money.

They exited at the rear of the building and again the brilliant sunshine blinded them as they emerged. They realized that they had come to the western-most edge of the park and that no more exhibits were displayed here. The disused amphitheater was further up the hill and they peeked into the deserted stage, now the province of weeds and unwanted, broken statues.

They wandered slowly back to the main square, checking out the old exhibits. Most had their signs removed. The Ten Courts of Hell seemed to be the only thing left in use at this end of the park. Further up the hill, closer to the now off-limits villa, they came across the more modern exhibits, scenes of a long-gone Singapore. Police in the garb of the 30s and 40s were seen arresting miscreants. Women with skirts flying upwards in the wind and low-cut bodices enticed men into questionable doorways. Wads of bills, clutched in the hands of reprobates fleeing on decidedly out of date motorcycles, caught the attention of the men in blue, who seemed overwhelmed by the pervasiveness of the vice surrounding them.

Barbie stood in front of one of a dozen scenes and laughed. "Wine, women, gambling and drugs! Ahhh, I bet they are still with us, even in squeaky clean Singapore."

"You bet," answered Jon as he joined her. "Oh no, look at what Georgia's doing now?"

At the same time that Barbie and Jon noticed, so too did the uniformed guard they had met earlier. The sound of his whistle rent the air as Georgia slipped into a cubby hole in one of the exhibits.

"No, no madam. You cannot go exhibits," he shouted at Georgia as she emerged, smiling ingratiatingly at him.

"Oh, I'm sorry. I didn't realize that these were so special. I am just fascinated by them and I wanted a closer look. I love the way they are made," she gushed on and on. Between her bright smile, the tossing of her red gold hair and her unabashed admiration for the 'Magnificence' of the Haw Par Villa, the guard had no time to remonstrate with her. She smoothly moved away from the exhibit she had desecrated by entering and strolled alongside the series of scenes, pointing out her favorite themes.

Barbie helped by throwing her arm protectively around Georgia and gently led her towards the exit. "We just love this place, so unique, so special," Barbie said, as the three headed for the exit. She turned to the guard, "I'll bet you just loved this place as a child too. Which are your favorites? I'll bet the fleeing thieves on the motorcycles, or maybe the Battle of the Mice? And I'll betcha that's why you have a job here? Couldn't get enough of the place, too fascinating for words." Barbie kept up the patter until they were far away from the place of disobedience.

The guard followed them as they made their escape, moving surely and swiftly, both Georgia and Barbie talking the whole way down the hill towards the gate, not allowing the guard to remonstrate with them again. Jon walked beside the two women and grinned at the young man.

Barbie took notice of the construction equipment further up the hill and off to the side from the exhibits. She couldn't quite read the signs, but it appeared that the area contained offices, storage places and employee rooms. She thought of Georgia and her attempts to enter the Battle Box museum from the exit. She seemed to have a rebellious streak, a desire to go where she was not allowed to go or perhaps just a curiosity that would kill a cat. She fell behind Jon, Georgia and the guard as they made their way to the ornate gate.

As she turned her head to see the exhibits they had missed, she felt a presence behind her. She turned around. The old gardener that she had seen before, now walked slowly, directly behind her, carrying a pair of shears. She turned to face him. Their eyes met briefly, before the old man dropped his gaze. Debating whether to confront the man, Barbie stared at him as he slowly walked past her, down the hill toward the rest of her group. She walked quickly, passed him and joined her companions.

"Are we ready to go? I'll bet our fellow here would like us to go now, yes?" Barbie said with a chirp.

She turned to Georgia and under her breath whispered, "Don't look now." She knew, of course, that any command like this was sure to elicit the opposite reaction. "We're being followed."

Sure enough, Georgia turned to look behind them. "What? Where?" she asked.

Barbie turned and was about to point out the gardener. But there was no one. And no sign that anyone had been there.

Chapter Eighteen: The Port of Singapore

Barbie turned to face Georgia. "He was right behind me. He was posing as a gardener. But he was no gardener; he was following us."

"What did he look like?" Georgia asked.

"He was dressed as a gardener. Short, 50-60ish. Flat cap, baggy coveralls, dirty gray-green. The first time I saw him he was wheeling a wheelbarrow. The second time he was carrying some clippers. Didn't either of you see him?" Barbie slowed and made sure the guard had stayed behind as they approached the exit.

"What made you think he was following us?" Georgia asked. "Maybe he was just a gardener."

"NO, NO. I know when I am being followed, and he was doing that. He was too casual, too obvious, too…" Barbie faltered.

"Jon, did you see him?" Georgia persisted. "Did you see the ersatz gardener following us?"

"I didn't see anyone but the patrol-type guard character. No one else was there." Jon shrugged in apology.

"I am NOT making things up. He was there. It is such a perfect cover," Barbie whined.

"Let's go, there is something else I want to show you. I really wish Matt would call again. I'm sure he will. And give us better directions." Georgia slowly sauntered past the entrance kiosk and waved to the man who sat in the booth with nothing to do. He waved back.

As they entered the parking lot, they turned to see the guard who had hassled them standing in the middle of the walkway. He folded his arms and scowled at them.

"Bye," Georgia waved gaily. "See you again!!"

Barbie noted that clouds had gathered and where there had been bright sunlight, it was now cloudy, with a breeze that whirled and twisted the dust, leaves and debris into eddies around the edges of the car park. Three empty plastic water bottles joined the trash fray and rattled in the still empty space.

"This place seems so disused, so deserted compared to other parts of Singapore," Jon remarked.

Ahead of them was the wide black maw of the Haw Par Villa MRT station. To their right was a wide busy street and to the left was the hillside of the Villa. Grass, some left long and uncut grew underneath towering trees and shorter shrubs. Georgia stopped, looked all around her and then swiftly headed into the wooded wilderness. Barbie and Jon scrambled quickly after her.

Within a minute of their scramble, they approached the wall that surrounded the Villa. Georgia found a space with slightly flattened grass and sat, her back against the wall. Barbie and Jon followed her lead. They had a view of the parking lot, the road, the entryway to the MRT, but were out of view of the entrance to Tiger Balm Gardens. They were inconspicuous.

Georgia found her water bottle and drank deeply. She stared straight ahead. "He brought me here, I think to this very spot, with the grass mashed down. We sat. He had brought some snacks and drinks. And we had a little picnic, sitting right here. I didn't quite know why he brought me. Maybe we were waiting for someone, just casually. I thought at first that we were here because of the MRT station, you can see the entrance, or exit, from here. But later I decided that maybe it was that," she pointed. In front of them, across the wide boulevard, was an enormous gate, bounded on both sides by large buildings. A slow, but steady stream of cars, small trucks and large trucks with trailers made their way in and out as the trio watched. "He said something strange. He said, 'Maybe tomorrow night.' I asked him what he meant and he didn't answer, only smiled. That was Matt, just giving out dribs and drabs of information. I think he was talking about something or someone arriving at the port. You know that ships take longer than trucks or ground transportation. And it doesn't matter whether they arrive today or tomorrow as much as it does getting your shipment 'safely to port'. I think he was waiting for a shipment. And perhaps someone to deliver it."

The three of them looked at the massive structure that could be seen beyond the entrance gates of the port of Singapore. From the road, the parts of the port that were visible were: the road, twisting in a 'keyhole' entrance, rather than entering directly, the large buildings and a small car park off to the right. From their vantage point, the trio could see over the buildings at the front to the ships and docksides beyond. Massive ocean-going freighters lined up for hundreds of meters out to sea and the deep boom of their active voices could be heard in the viscera as well as the ear.

"Gold?" Jon asked. "Was he waiting for a shipment of gold?"

"Remember, 'jin' means other things as well. It could have been those stupid fake Viagra drugs as far as I know." Georgia scowled at the thought.

"Could it have been real drugs, heroin or something?" Jon asked.

"Never, he was not that stupid. They still hang people for drug offenses in Singapore." Georgia's shoulders fell. "He loved the cloak and dagger stuff: the hiding, the secret meetings, the code words. I think he felt 'manly' by doing something dangerous, outwitting someone, especially the authorities, making some money. The fake Viagra I can see. It's illegal, but it's not addictive and not really dangerous. If he were to be caught, he might be expelled, but certainly not hung."

They fell silent and watched the clouds gather, filling the sky. The wind picked up even more and the temperature fell slightly.

Georgia took her phone, checked to see that there was still some battery left. "Call, Matt, call me," she said to the blank screen.

"Why are you so sure he will call you? Did he say he would call?" Barbie ventured timidly.

"No, it was very short, cryptic, just like him."

"Why exactly did he say?" Barbie asked.

"He started off like he sometimes did, he said, 'Hi Ginger.' That was a special pet name for me. You know, red hair and all." She put her head back and rolled her eyes. "I wish I had never taught him that name. I never liked being ginger-haired. I asked him not to call me that, as a matter of fact. And then he said, 'Miss you. Go to Haw Par Villa, look for 'jin''. That's all. Maybe something else, but I didn't hear it. The connection was bad, and there was background noise."

Barbie leaned forward and tentatively asked, in a voice barely above a whisper. "Just a thought, but… Are you sure it was Matt? The voice, the accent, the grammar? Was it really him?"

"Of course, it was him, he called me 'Ginger'!" Georgia shot back.

"But you said you asked him not to do that. Why would he call you a name you didn't like?" Barbie persisted.

"Well… Maybe it was a bit weird, maybe he forgot??" Georgia stopped then and bowed her head.

"Or maybe someone else had overheard him and thought it was your 'pet' name. Used it to fool you? How clear was the connection? How sure are you?" Barbie continued. "Could you recognize his voice, or just thought you could?"

"No, I really didn't 'recognize' his voice," she answered slowly. "And another thing, he said, 'Haw Par Villa'. We always called it the Tiger Balm Gardens. I mean, they mean the same thing, everyone knows that. Did he say Haw Par Villa?" Georgia asked.

"You repeated that during your conversation. Remember, I asked you what it was?" Barbie said.

"Yeah, I did. I guess I just assumed it was him. Maybe it wasn't." Georgia's voice began to quaver.

"Or maybe it was him, but he was being coerced? Are you sure there was no number?"

Georgia looked at her phone once more and shook her head, "No number."

While Georgia and Barbie were having this conversation, Jon had wandered off and looked at the hillside, the wall, and the grass at his feet. He returned to where they sat and asked Georgia, "Are you sure this is the exact place you sat before?"

"Pretty sure. See, the grass is beaten down. Matt had brought a little mat thing, you know, for the beach? We sat on that. That's why I came here, because I thought maybe I could get some ideas by looking at what we looked at before. And see, the grass is still bent over, a little. Why do you ask?"

"The wall is lower here. I think it would be an easy climb for me up onto the wall. And probably Matt could as well, with a little help. He wasn't particularly short, was he?" Jon asked. "With a little leg up from a friend? Care to try?"

Barbie looked at the wall for the first time. Nearer the entrance, the white stucco walls were topped with elaborate tiles, but here, the construction crew had short changed the architect by using inferior material. The top was not tile, but adobe-colored stucco, rounded at the top. From a distance, no one could tell.

Georgia stood, brushing the dry grass from her backside. Barbie, too, stood to watch what her son and friend were about to do.

Jon chose a spot that was level on the outside and a person could easily stand, hands braced to help an accomplice to the top of the wall. Georgia made a cup with her hands and dug in her heels. Jon gently put his foot in her hands and tried to position his hands and arms to grab the top of the wall when he leapt.

"One, two, three," Georgia counted.

Jon flew upwards and grabbed the top of the wall, pulling himself up easily. He straddled the top and grinned down at Georgia and Barbie. "Success," he said cockily.

"Where are you?" Georgia asked.

"Twenty-five feet from the exit of the Courts of Hell. Not all that far from where you saw the 'jin' sign." He smiled down at them. He then looked out towards the port. "Great view from up here. You can see the entrance quite clearly. All the ships lined up, everything."

"Gruff, gruff, woof, woof." The muffled sound came from the far side of the wall, followed by scrabbling sounds.

Barbie looked up to see Jon's face go white and then heard a yelping sound from his throat. "Shit, German shepherd. Coming down," he announced as he motioned for them to move away from the wall in preparation for his leap down.

He landed with a 'whoof' of breath and a grumble. "Didn't see that coming at all!"

"Just the dog?" Georgia asked. "No disgruntled guard?"

"Don't know, didn't stay long enough to find out. Actually, I don't think he could have reached me, but he took me by surprise, came out of nowhere. Wooow."

"I think it's time to leave," Barbie announced, as she bent to pick up her bag which she had left on the ground. A rumble from the distance caused her to look up. Banks of racing black and gray clouds swirled in the air above them.

"MRT station," Georgia said. "I think it might rain and I didn't bring my umbrella." She stowed her phone, picked up her bag and started down the hill, in a direct line.

Barbie followed, sliding on the slick grass. Jon grabbed her arm at one point, helping her slide more gently down. As they entered the parking lot, Georgia turned to them. "Don't look now," she laughed, "Our friends are watching." She pointed to the entrance of the park. Standing on the steep entrance ramp were the guard they had met earlier, the man from the entrance kiosk and a large German shepherd, growling and prancing at the end of a leash.

"Go," said Barbie, pushing Jon and Georgia from behind. "Time to leave." A gust of wind tore at her words, but none needed to be told to hurry towards the station.

Another burst of wind flailed at them, thrusting bits of leaves and dust in their eyes as it swirled around the empty lot. Barbie stopped to wipe her eyes and as she opened them a brilliant flash of light was quickly followed by a piercing boom that seemed to fill her entire body. She screamed.

As she took a shaky breath, she could smell a harsh metallic stench that overlay the dust. Ahead of her, she could see Georgia and Jon, who had also stopped at the closeness of the lightning strike. Georgia's short red hair stood up around her head like a bloody halo. "Run," she called to them, "rain!"

Barbie forced her legs into action just as the water began to fall from the sky. The rain fell not in drops, but in cupfuls, in bucketfuls, like a broken showerhead turned on full force. Her feet squelched in the puddles that formed instantaneously on the uneven pavement. Her hair, soaked within ten seconds of the shower, ran in rivulets in her eyes, keeping her from seeing where she was headed. Only the thought of an even closer lightning strike kept her moving.

At the entrance to the MRT station, Jon and Georgia waited for her. Although damp, they seemingly had escaped the worst of the sudden rain shower. While Barbie stood dripping, creating a small lake around her ankles, they shook droplets of moisture from their shoulders. She gave both of them a look of incredulity. How come it is always ME that gets the short end of the stick?

Georgia glowered over Barbie's shoulder and looked daggers out the entrance. "Time to go," she announced.

Jon found an extra shirt in his bag, handed it to his mother and helped her dry the worst of the rain off. "Okay now, Mom?" he asked sympathetically. He turned to follow Georgia into the station.

Barbie sighed and straightened. She looked ahead of her with determination and began to walk slowly towards the trains. Within a few steps, she stopped and her mouth opened in amazement. A short figure, dressed in coveralls, stood with his back to her and faced the ATM. Barbie kept moving, never letting her gaze falter. As she neared the machine, the short man turned to look at her. Their eyes met, again. He blinked, then turned to focus on his business.

This time, Barbie took time to press the image into her memory. This time, she would not forget the face, nor the stance, nor that she had seen him twice today. Was he just going home from work? Or was he following them?

Chapter Nineteen: A Visit to Mrs. Lee

On the train ride, Barbie tried to tell Georgia and Jon about the man who was following them, but neither had the time to listen. They had not seen anyone, they declared, and that was the end of the story as far as they were concerned. Barbie then fell into silence, nursing hurt feelings for not being believed. *Did I really see him, or was I making something up?* She recalled looking into his eyes. *No, I did see the same man and I didn't like the look in his eyes.*

Georgia and Barbie sat together with Jon hanging by a strap near them. Georgia looked around to see if anyone was paying attention. "I want to visit Mrs. Lee," she said.

"You want to go back to Matt's apartment?" Barbie hissed.

"No, I want to see her. It's near Matt's place. I saw her one day going into a door and Matt said that was where she lived. I think I can find it again. If all else fails, I have her number, remember?"

Barbie looked closely at her friend. Georgia seemed quiet and calm. Determined to have her way.

They got off at Chinatown and by now Barbie was thoroughly cool from the air conditioning in the train; she shivered until they exited the station and met the warm air outside. One brilliant flash of late afternoon sun nearly blinded them as they descended the walkway onto Pagoda Street. The evening crowd had started to gather, tiptoeing around puddles in the street. Barbie shook her head, "A half hour ago, it was raining cats and dogs, and now, sunshine and puddles." Even as they walked, the street began to fill and before they reached the first turning to Matt's apartment, they had begun to push and shove their way through.

Near the end of the block, Georgia stopped in front of a phone store. She peered inside and then pushed the door open. In the center of the store was a massive central pillar. Georgia circled it, picking up one, then another, of the cords that dangled from it. She fished out her phone, plugged it in to a free cord of the right kind, and laid her phone down with half a dozen other phones similarly being charged. She went to the counter in the back of the tiny shop and spoke softly to the uniformed girl standing there. Barbie saw her slip the girl a note and there was a firm nod. She turned to her friends, "We have time to visit Mrs. Lee. She'll watch the phone and answer if it rings."

"You're leaving your phone with a total stranger. What if Matt calls again? Do you think this is wise?" Barbie questioned.

Georgia shrugged, "What choice do I have?" She led the way, initially towards Matt's apartment, but stopped one alleyway short.

"What's the address?" Jon asked.

"I dunno. I will know when I get there." She continued slowly down the deserted alleyway, looking to right and left, occasionally turning around and eyeing the doors from the opposite direction.

"What a novel way to find your way around. I'd rather use my GPS," Jon remarked, following Georgia closely.

"Here, I think," Georgia said stopping in front of a nondescript alley door. She looked around, stepped back five or six steps and looked again. "Yep, I'm sure." She rang the bell.

They held their collective breath and listened for signs of life. Georgia pressed the doorbell again, then leaned in and listened at the door, ear pressed against it.

"Third time's a charm," she said, pressing the doorbell insistently.

The door made noises as if a latch were unlocked. A tiny sliver of dark interior showed. An eyeball pressed to the opening.

"Mrs. Lee, it's me, Matt's friend. I'm so glad to find you at home. I was wondering if you had seen Matt yet?"

"No, no see." The voice came softly with a husky undertone.

"Well, he's come back. I'm sure he'll come back to his apartment soon. And I am sure that he would like to find his apartment clean. I hope you haven't let anyone else in that apartment. It's still nice and clean like I left it, isn't it?"

"I don't know what you talk," came the almost garbled reply.

"There are lots of keys out there, you know you can't always tell how a key has been used." Georgia leaned in closely. "Nice and clean? No one else been there?"

"Too many keys. I don't know," Mrs. Lee whispered.

"Yes, you do know what I'm talking about. You know that someone else was there. Now that Matt is back, it was just a short trip, you have the responsibility, don't you?" Georgia pressed.

"Not my job. He dirty place, his job," Mrs. Lee spit out.

"It is your responsibility to see to your apartments. Maybe I should call the police?" Georgia threatened.

"You call police, they arrest him!" she said angrily.

"Maybe they'll arrest you too!" came Georgia's reply. "I think you need to make the apartment the way he left it. Remember, I paid the rent for him. It's your job to make sure everything works, is clean, is okay. I won't call the police if you do your job!"

The door had opened wider and now Barbie could see both of Mrs. Lee's eyes. They narrowed and the look she gave Georgia was not a pleasant one. She said nothing.

"By the way, who did you let in?" Georgia asked.

The door slammed with a resounding thud and the three sleuths were once more alone in the alleyway.

"Well, at least I know she let someone in, but also that she will go back and maybe clean it up a bit. I hope she doesn't throw things away." Georgia led the way back to the phone store.

Georgia spoke briefly to the girl behind the counter, unplugged her phone and paid. "If it's not fully charged, it's a lot better than before. And he didn't call. I let the girl know that if he did call, she was to tell him to call back in 15 minutes, but..." she sighed deeply.

"Can we go to Geylang, now?" Jon asked tentatively. "I don't think anyone will be there until it's really 'dark' and it's just dusk now. Yannis said we could meet him there, after dark."

"Let's go slowly. We can take a stroll and catch the MRT from Outram Park. It's straight from there. Ummmm," Georgia mused. "Have you ever had Hainanese Chicken Rice?"

"More food!" Barbie whined. "You are going to fatten me up."

"The Singapore tourist experience is all about food. Great food here, don't you think? As the 'piece de resistance', we can go to the Tiffin Room at Raffles for high tea!" Georgia babbled on, to herself, as Barbie looked at the goods for sale at the street-side kiosks. Gaudy trinkets made from ersatz silk in brilliant colors and styles waylaid her so that Jon had to continually backtrack and rescue her.

Georgia ducked into a tiny restaurant between two shops and went to the counter in the rear. Soon they were seated and Georgia was taking their preferences for drinks. "Orange or lemon, I think. If you want Coke or something, it's extra. It's cheap enough, even if you don't drink the cheap stuff."

They had barely had a chance to taste their drinks, served in the flimsiest plastic glasses Barbie had ever used, when three plates were plonked down in front of them. A quarter of a chicken, a generous mound of rice and a few shreds of cabbage with dressing constituted the specialty of the house. The skin on the chicken, glistening with oil, was pale yellowish white. The rice was delicately flavored with gleaming white chunks of garlic and a sprinkling of some yellowish condiment. The salad, white cabbage with approximately three strands of purple, exhibited the only color on the plate. The smell was heavenly, even to the supposedly satiated Barbie.

Around them, Singaporeans shoveled chicken into their mouths with great gusto, eyeing the foreigners, waiting to see how they would 'appreciate' one of Singapore's signature dishes. Despite herself, Barbie found the food went down smoothly. Soon, they were wiping their lips and fingers with tiny rough napkins and asking for a refill on their drinks.

Barbie sat companionably beside Jon and gave him a little bump. He bumped back. "Did I tell you how glad I am that we met up here? And I am terribly sorry for all the times we missed each other. I want to let you know that even though it was not always my fault, I did try to avoid you. I was afraid."

Jon looked uncomfortable, but tried to focus on the conversation, "Afraid of what?"

"Afraid you'd blame me, say I was a bad mother for leaving you and going off to see the world."

"You weren't a bad mom. You had to live your own life!" Jon said generously.

"I could have taken you with me."

"I didn't know that you ever offered," Jon looked at her in surprise.

"I didn't offer, I just said I could have. I was a little mad at you, and maybe taking revenge."

"Revenge?"

"I felt rejected because you wanted to live with your father."

"A boy needs his father."

"Yours is a flake, a total flake, not good enough to be a father."

"He loves me." Jon turned to Barbie. "As hard as that is for you to take, he does love me."

"I just hope that living with him didn't do you any harm. I worried about that. Did he teach you any bad habits?"

Jon laughed. "Naaw, none that were permanent. A little smoking, a little drinking. Man stuff."

Barbie sighed.

"Listen Mom, I needed him in my life at that time."

"Your grandfather would have taught you a little smoking and a little drinking. He could have done that, you didn't need that…"

"Don't say anything you might regret."

"I feel like you rejected me, so I pushed you away."

"I didn't feel that way. We kept in touch, all those skype talks."

"But I should have been there for you, like he was. He was there!"

"No, he wasn't. He's a flake. YOU were there. Remember all my girlfriends?"

"Yeah, you seemed to have a lot of them, I worried that you weren't being able to settle down with anyone. And it was my fault, for not being there," Barbie bit her lip, trying not to cry.

"No, you met them ALL, every girl I ever looked at. I was so afraid I'd make a mistake, or that you hadn't met them and liked them, that I insisted you meet them. Some of them were just study friends, but you met them all. And Dad, well, he didn't meet any of them. None. I only introduced them to you. I trusted your judgement, not his."

Barbie's eyes started to fill with tears and she wiped at them ineffectually with the thin, slick papers.

"You're my mom, you're my rock!" Jon said, bumping Barbie again.

"Sorry to break up this love fest, but it's getting to be time to go." Georgia started gathering her things, stowing her phone into an inside pocket in her pack. "And Barbie, I have never heard you talk that way about your ex. Sounds like you have trouble picking good men. Is this another case, like in Turkey, picking bad 'uns?"

 Phyllis Wachob

"Look who's talking? Tell me about picking good men! It's your boyfriend who has gone missing? Who chooses boyfriends like that anyway?" Barbie hissed.

"Ladies, ladies," Jon intervened. "There are some good men in the world. I admit that my Dad is not one of the terribly good ones, but I'm sure Matt has his good points. Look, it's dark." He pointed to the sky, now purple-black. "We need to find Bruce Lee. Something tells me that he is important, or that his knowledge is."

Chapter Twenty: Search for Bruce Lee

As they were already close to the MRT station, their transition to Aljumied station, only seven stops away in the Geylang district of Singapore, was easy. When they exited the station, Barbie expected the neighborhood to be substantially different from other places in Singapore. After all, this place was a known red-light district. But she was surprised to find that it looked quite normal, if a little on the poor and run-down side. A short two block walk, through dimly lighted streets, brought them to Geylang Road. Barbie assumed the poor lighting was the norm throughout the world on the theory that municipal governments do not pay a lot to light poor areas, only wealthy ones. The wide boulevard sported well-lit shops on both sides of the road, with pedestrian traffic that looked within international norms.

"Are you sure we're in the right place? I don't see any, you know, around here," Barbie asked Georgia and Jon.

"I think that the women, male prostitutes are not allowed, are all inside. It's not legal to solicit, so these women should not be prostitutes," answered Georgia. "Not that I know a lot about it."

"Yannis told me that Bruce Lee would be hanging around the corner of Geylang Road and Lorong 16 or 18, which are on that side of the Road. Maybe he'd be on this side, the odd numbered lorongs," Jon reported.

"What are lorongs?" Barbie asked,

"Alleys, or lanes or NOT roads. Especially in this part of Singapore, there are lots of little streets in the back, with no given names, just numbers." Georgia said.

"And the even numbered lorongs are where the brothels are, the odd numbered lorongs are for respectable people," Jon said. "So I was told."

"In that case, the woman sitting there, is just respectable?" Barbie asked, pointing at a woman sitting at a cold drink shop on a tiny stool. She flipped through a magazine and sipped on a straw stuck in a plastic cup.

The three stared at her until she looked up at them. Jon smiled; she didn't smile back. Georgia gave Barbie a push and they walked further along Geylang Road, reading the lorong numbers.

"Lorong 23, 21," Barbie read. "I think we are on the wrong side of the street. These are all the odd numbered ones." She peered down the street. "No red lights."

They kept walking until they were opposite the even numbered lorongs between 16 and 18. "This is it," said Jon.

They stood on the street corner. After a minute, Georgia said in a conspiratorial undertone. "I feel conspicuous, very. What are WE doing here? We look totally out of place."

"Cold drink," said Jon, pointing to a simple stand that sold cold drinks and snacks just twenty feet from the corner. Small stools stood to the side, welcoming patrons. They bought local exotic flavors of fizzy drinks in small bottles. Barbie giggled at the names of Shark and Pink Dolphin and gawked at the intensely orange colored one.

The owner put a straw in each one and gestured towards the stools. "Empty bottle, here" he said as Jon paid, indicating a stack of wooden crates with cubby holes for returned bottles.

Barbie gasped in delight. "I haven't seen anything like that in years, not since I was a kid. Is this cheap or is this ecologically friendly?"

They sat and drank their sodas and watched the scene. Barbie watched the less than clean-cut men lounge around the street corner. Within minutes more of them arrived and from behind trees, small kiosks and from the alleys, wooden fruit crates appeared. Squares made from parts of boxes or stiff cardboard were placed on top and over that, a small white sheet. These small display tables gradually came to life in only a few minutes. The men produced, out of small bags hung on their shoulders, a variety of boxes, packages and pouches laid out neatly in rows. The colorful displays were individual, but contained the same basic variety of goods.

Barbie watched as Jon sauntered over to look at the nearest display. He picked up one package that was bright red, with gold lettering and a logo. The writing was too far away for Barbie to read, but she thought these might be the fake Viagra and the men, the sellers, friends of Bruce Lee's. And Matt's friends, or customers, if indeed he was involved in this trade. Jon was working his 'manly' charm on the guy. They traded good natured jokes, then the seller nodded towards Jon's two women. The jokes turned a little too risqué for Barbie, who couldn't hear them, she could only read the body language.

Barbie leaned over to Georgia, who had stood to return her drink bottle to the case, "I hope that he realizes, or maybe not, that I'm Jon's mother."

"Ah, all ang mos, white people, look alike. They'd never guess." Georgia inched closer to hear the conversation.

Barbie was startled, "Is that what they say? That we all look the same? That can't be true!"

"Are you surprised? White people aren't the only racists in the world. Here comes Jon. Let's see what he's found out." Georgia joined Jon, who casually walked away from the seller, slipping something in his pocket.

"The guy said that Bruce Lee would surely be around later. He suggested we go have some fruit, at the durian stand. Said durian gives 'power', just as good as his medicine. He said it was down this way." Jon plunged into yet another darkened side street.

Barbie could smell the durian stand before she could see it. The sickly-sweet rotten smell of putrefying fruit wafted towards her nostrils. They turned a corner and in front of them, displayed in glorious ascending banks in the cases, were the durian. The wildly varying prices reflected the variety and quality of the fruit. The one thing they had in common was their spiky skin, although the size varied from the size of a grapefruit to monstrous elongated watermelons. Georgia laughed. "You know they call the Opera House and Concert Hall, near the harbor, the Durians. They look like two giant durians because of the spikes. You can also see signs in the buses, a durian with a red line through it. 'No durians allowed.' People have even been known to try and smuggle them onto planes, can you imagine? Oh, Singaporeans do love their stinky fruit!"

"Do you like it?" asked Barbie.

"No, not very much. It's interesting to taste, though. Ah, thank you sir," Georgia said as the owner brought a plate of fruit and placed in on a small table in the middle of the shop. The wrinkled greenish white pods were still in the skin, the two-inch long fingers nestling against one another, glistening with moisture, and exuding a delicate smell.

"Really, the smell's not too bad, interesting. How do I eat them, with my fingers?" Barbie asked.

"Better not, use one of these plastic papers so you don't get the oil on your skin," Georgia advised. "The smell stays a very long time."

"I had some durian ice cream in Hong Kong but I've never tasted the real thing," Jon said, using a paper to gently scoop one of the pods out of the skin. He bit into it, then slipped it all into his mouth and chewed.

Barbie watched and cautiously imitated her son. She successfully wrestled one finger from its bed and brought it to her mouth. She hesitated and began to smell it.

"No, eat first, don't smell," advised Georgia.

Barbie bit into the fruit which was firm, but gave easily to the pressure from her teeth. She chewed slowly and swallowed the small piece quickly. She brought the small pod to her mouth again, and then she smelled it. "Yuck," she squealed, pulling it away from her face. "Euwww, puke! Smells like, like, pig farm meets fruit garbage dump! Oh yuck." She thrust it away from her face and used her left hand to wipe her mouth. "Oh lordy, lordy, I ate some of it!"

Jon and Georgia laughed as Barbie tried to distance herself from the fruit in front of her. Jon continued to devour his piece and reached for Barbie's.

"Aren't you having any?" Barbie asked Georgia, who had quietly not taken any.

Georgia gave Barbie a slinky smirk. Barbie snorted in acknowledgment of Georgia's deception.

The owner laughed and approached the table with a pile of red and white chunks heaped on a small plate. "Dragon fruit," he said, placing it among them. "Foreigners like." Dragon fruit turned out to be a sweet juicy fruit with tiny black seeds spread equidistant throughout. The flesh of one kind was white and another ruby red. Barbie dived into the dragon fruit and both the women let Jon finish the durian. The owner tried to sell them a whole durian, but knew there was no way they were going to get it home undetected by the MRT riders.

"Let's see if Bruce Lee has shown up yet," Jon suggested.

They retraced their steps and arrived back at the street corner with the fake Viagra sellers, about twenty in all, each jealously guarding their own bit of turf. Jon spoke with the man he had approached before. He joined the two women who were once again hovering near the cold drink seller.

"Apparently, Bruce Lee has been and gone. He is checking on his 'other' businesses. I think it is some sort of gambling thing. The guy said he would be back in a while. What do we do, wait?" Jon consulted with Georgia.

Georgia answered by shrugging and rolling her eyes.

Before any decision could be made, confusion erupted around them. A short whistle blast, hardly more than a loud tweet, caused the fake Viagra sellers to stir into action. Barbie could not see what was happening, but she sensed a whirlwind of white sheets being grabbed, a toppling of boxes and then they were gone, the sellers and their goods. She looked around her and she could see none of them, nothing of their packets and boxes of aphrodisiacs. Where one minute before there had been a lively display and a thriving market, now there was nothing but a few wooden boxes scattered on the ground.

"What happened?" asked Barbie. "Where did they go? And why?"

Jon nodded towards Geylang Road, where just a scant half block away, two handsome young men in spotless police uniforms sauntered nonchalantly along the sidewalk. Their heads swiveled gently from side to side, but they did not exude any menacing vibes. In fact, one laughed at something said by the other. They smiled at the drinks seller. They must have seen the detritus of the deserted fake Viagra market, but made no outward sign of anything amiss.

Barbie watched the police and then felt Georgia standing very close behind her, breathing shallowly. Was Georgia alarmed? Nervous? Was this police presence a threat to them? To Bruce Lee? To the missing Matt?

Chapter Twenty-one: The Police

"What was that all about?" Barbie whispered. The others, the fruit seller, the drink seller and pedestrians around them, went about their business in a very unconcerned mode. But the absence of the men, who had been selling dubious goods and who had escaped the threat of fines or even jail, hung over the corner.

"Look," Jon indicated the policemen who were now strolling further up the street in a jocular mood. "It looks like no one was interested in making arrests."

Georgia looked after the police and then remarked, "Someone tipped the fake Viagra sellers off. They disappeared so quickly, so efficiently and in just the nick of time. If the police saw them, they would have had to do something about it. It's as if there is 'secret' communication between the bad 'uns and the good 'uns. I get the impression that the police do NOT want to catch the fake medicine sellers."

"I think they have lookouts," Jon replied. "I think they'll be back when the police have well and truly gone."

Georgia looked around, "Uh, let's go somewhere a bit more private, we need to talk." Jon indicated with his head the opposite side of the street where the lorong disappeared into blackness just a few feet from the road.

When they had crossed the road, and stood in the shadows, Georgia said, "Call Yannis. I thought he was supposed to meet us here and help us look for Bruce Lee. Where is he?"

Jon walked off a few feet and the two women could see him talking into the phone, gesticulating as he spoke.

"Why does he think he has to talk privately?" Georgia asked.

"I think it's a guy thing, they want to say snide things about us to one another, but don't want us to hear."

Soon Jon returned and pointed down the lorong. "Gambling is down this way, maybe Bruce Lee went there. He has 'business interests' in the gambling games."

"Where's Yannis?" asked Georgia.

"Oh, he got hung up. He said to call him anytime if we get lost or need any more information. He is sure that Bruce Lee will be here, somewhere. But he didn't offer to give me Bruce Lee's number. And I didn't like to ask." Jon shrugged. "Actually, I know that Mom has it, so if we really need it…"

"What if Bruce Lee gets picked up by the police?" Barbie asked.

"They all know by now. There are lookouts on the main corners. Look there's one now." Jon used his head to indicate a man sitting on a tiny plastic stool near the corner. Barbie could just see the ear bud and a cord that ran deep into his shirt and was undoubtedly hooked up to a phone. The man could see up and down the street and make notes on who came through the narrow entrance to the back street. If the police made a U-turn or made another sweep down Geylang Road, he would be on his phone, sending messages to other lookouts of illegal activities.

Jon suggested, "Let's take a look down here at the gambling and try to find Bruce Lee. And if we don't find him, we can come back in 20 or 25 minutes. That should give everybody enough time to return."

Barbie looked down the dark alleyway and wondered what was there. Gambling, Jon said. But what if it wasn't? What if it was gambling, but of the unsavory kind? Is this something I shouldn't be doing? This last thought, that someone might tell Barbie what she couldn't do, sent her following her son and her friend into the dark.

Street lamps threw faint circles of light onto the uneven ground of the alley. Barbie saw one pole that had no light. Was this the result of dubious municipal services again, or was it put out by the gamblers, wanting to hide their nefarious deeds? Ahead she saw a brilliant light, but at head height, so it must be private. Her view of it was blocked by a small crowd, their heads bent over something. As they drew nearer, Barbie peeked over the heads of the players and looked at the gaming board. Like the fake Viagra sellers, the whole apparatus was homemade. A large white sheet lay on a makeshift table, about five by eight feet. Black paint had been used to mark out squares, and Chinese characters painted in them. A marker was being waved about and Barbie didn't have any sense of what the game was about. The players were all men, dressed in nondescript clothes that might have been second hand or worn for many moons. They wore dirty plastic flip-flops or plastic shoes. Small bills were being waved about and the men talked urgently amongst themselves. Jon looked around the crowd and then asked someone who looked like another lookout. Barbie watched as the man shook his head. The man pointed down the alley away from Geylang Road. Oh dear, deeper into the belly of the beast.

"Did the guy know who you were looking for?" Barbie asked Jon as they made their way carefully down the poorly lit alley, avoiding piles of trash and potholes.

"Yeah, they all know Bruce Lee. I had no idea how popular he was, or how well-known. The reason why we are going this way is because he was spotted going here. Something about delivering goods to one of the houses."

"You know, I feel really conspicuous about being a woman here, there haven't been any other women around," Barbie said.

"Ah, I think that is about to change. The 'houses' up this way are the brothels," said Jon as they came to a corner of a more brightly lit street.

The houses here looked like suburbia, without the front lawns. They were two-storied with deep driveways. The fronts were brightly lit and many had large blinking house numbers. The predominant color was red, but green, orange, yellow, and all colors of the rainbow blended in for a carnival atmosphere. The only jarring note seemed to be the lavish Buddhist shrines that stood near the entrance to each building. The gold miniature Buddhas and attendant twinkling lights, red tassels and accoutrements seemed to be out of place to the 'Christianized' foreigners. Barbie thought she was taught to think of brothels as vice, and shrines to a deity an opposition to this 'sin'. But obviously, people here had a different cultural orientation.

As they walked slowly, taking in the gaudy lights and flashy cars crawling along the street, Barbie craned her neck to peek into the houses of ill-repute. She glimpsed a 'fish-bowl' room in the second house. In it, lavishly made up young women, or made up to look young, lounged in a pastel painted room. The couch was lavender and the walls painted pale blue. Their clothes covered their bodies to entice men inside. One woman wore a dress with a wide flouncy yellow skirt, that pinched her waist, and a tight bodice. Another wore tiger printed yoga pants and a gauzy shirt. One flipped through a magazine, the other texted on her phone; no one made eye contact with the customers. If a man wanted anything, he needed to go inside and pay to get any action.

Jon stopped in front of one house and approached an old man sitting in the driveway, next to the Buddhist shrine. He asked Jon a few questions, trying to entice him in. Then he spotted the two women.

"Tourist go away. No good place tourist," he shouted at them.

Georgia stood straight and glared. "Why do I have to go away? I can go where I want!"

"No good. Tourist lady no good. Polis catch, big trouble!" he answered.

"Why me? Your ladies don't get arrested, do they?" Georgia countered.

"This ladies medical certificate. You not have, you big trouble. Go away, go away. Polis come, big trouble." The old man came out to the edge of the driveway in a menacing stance.

Georgia and Barbie backed away, not understanding the reason why the man was so aggressive, but not willing to counter him. They watched from the end of the driveway as Jon spoke to him some more. Barbie heard nothing until an outburst from the old man.

"Bruce Lee? No here, no here," the man said, spitting on the ground. "Low class…" His outburst ended with a string of Chinese, presumably curses.

Jon backed away and joined the women and they slowly made their way down the street, away from the angry brothel guardian. "I don't think Bruce Lee is very popular around this part of Geylang. And I found out why he was so anxious for you two to move off. The women in the brothels all have medical certificates and the police occasionally come in to check. If they found one of you inside, with no medical certificate, the owner would be in trouble, and his brothel closed down. They are understandably anxious not to have strange women around. Let's head back towards the fake Viagra marketplace. At least there, they know him and don't yell at us to go away."

They turned around and Barbie realized that across the street from the two-story brothels was an eight-story hotel. "Whoa, a hotel, here?"

Georgia immediately had her phone out. "Hah," she laughed, "a flea-bag at $45 Singapore a night. Or maybe that's per hour!"

Just as she remarked on the dubious nature of the hotel, a sleek, dark expensive car glided up to the well-lit entrance. A woman emerged from the back seat, her long legs barely encased in a very short black sequined skirt. She flipped her waist length black hair out of the way, as she hitched a matching sequined purse onto her shoulder. An awkward high-heeled mincing stride took her to the door and quickly inside. The car glided away.

"Delivery," Georgia commented.

"Like pizza? Call up and order your favorite?" Barbie added. "Let's find Bruce Lee and get out of here. This is no longer interesting or cute, just sleazy. It's beginning to depress me."

"Polis, polis," came a cry from one of the driveway attendants up the street. Barbie turned towards the commotion and saw the man run into the street, waving his arms.

An outpouring of men burst from the gambling alleyway, running helter-skelter. "Run, run," one young man said to them as he sped past. "Polis, polis."

Barbie grabbed Georgia's arm and pulled. "Hide, we have to find a place to hide. We can't be caught here!!" Directly in front of her and off to the right, across the intersection, was a dark corner, sheltered from the street lights by tall trees, which cast deep shadows. "There, let's get under the trees!"

Barbie pulled Georgia with her as they crossed the intersection and entered a dark patch under tall eucalyptus trees. The dry leaves crunched under their feet as they sought dark hiding spaces. Barbie tucked herself behind a tree and saw Georgia disappear into the bushes to her right. Barbie's heart pounded noisily, even as the cacophony of the gamblers grew quieter.

"Ow, let go. Stop," screamed Georgia from her hiding place.

An oomph, a crunch and a high-pitched male scream preceded a body which flew into the street and landed heavily near Barbie's feet.

"Ahhhhhh," screeched Georgia again.

Chapter Twenty-Two: Finding Bruce Lee

Barbie heard Georgia's screams close to her, although she couldn't see anything for the foliage that surrounded her. She was also shocked at the four-letter words that came out of Georgia's mouth, sailor's language her mother called it.

"Georgia, are you okay?" Barbie asked, not moving from her hiding place.

"Listen you, no one, but no one touches me unless I say so. Do you get it?" Georgia spoke, obviously not in answer to Barbie's question.

Barbie peeked out and saw, in the dim light from down the street, a figure on the ground and Georgia standing over it. She looked in the opposite direction, that of the previous commotion, but all was quiet, far too quiet. All the gamblers had fled and the some of the houses had turned off their flashing lights. "Are you okay," Barbie asked again.

The figure on the ground stood and backed away from the glowering Georgia, all the while adjusting a towering wig of strawberry blond curls. "You're not ladyboy," said a distinctly masculine voice.

"Of course, I'm not a ladyboy, why did you think that?" came the swift reply.

"But, but this place, this place is…" the overdressed figure said. "This place is not for ladies. You should go up there," he said, pointing up the street towards the brothels. He inched around Georgia and tried to press himself back into the shadows, while smoothing his fuchsia mini-skirt.

"I think he's trying to say that we are the trespassers in this part of the street, that this place is for the other kind of ladies of the night," Barbie said, trying to placate the angry Georgia.

"Yeah, I guess so," she answered. "the Singaporean government is not fond of the gay scene, always trying to push it back into the shadows." She turned to the cowering figure in the deep shadows. "But you! I don't care if you are straight or gay – you have to ask first! Hands to yourself."

"Sorry, sorry," the erstwhile groper said, adjusting his clothes as he inched away and prepared to leave. "Sorry, sorry." He minced off down the street away from the brothels, teetering on his high heels.

"I have a feeling he may be new to this," Barbie said. "He's not too good with those five-inch heels."

"Who is? I don't even wear high heels anymore," Georgia said.

"I haven't even owned a pair for a good ten years!" Barbie added.

"Let's go find Jon. Hopefully he has found Bruce Lee by now." Georgia stepped out of the shadows and into the street, heading for the 'gambler's alley' and 'fake Viagra square'.

As they passed the hotel at the corner, a tour bus pulled up. As they watched, a stream of tourists, presumably Chinese, flooded out of the doors. The mostly middle-aged and elderly walked with tired steps, clutching bags full of shopping.

"Do they know what part of town they are in?" Barbie asked.

"Cheap hotel, remember?" Georgia answered. "Oh look, there's Jon."

Jon had joined the thin older man and was sitting on a tiny stool in front of the Buddha shrine while he chatted with the doormen. Barbie thought that of course Jon would be able to charm anyone; everyone was a friend to Jon. She thought of her father and wondered if Jon had gotten the trait of loveableness from him. Or he could have inherited the smooth-talker gene from his father. In any case, Jon could strike up a conversation with anyone and within minutes, they were friends.

Barbie hung back. Let him work his magic. He might be finding out things that are useful. Barbie pulled Georgia into the shadows of the tour bus to wait for an opportune moment.

Within a minute, Jon had spotted them. He broke off his conversation with the doorman, shook hands with the grinning man, waved and joined them in neutral ground in the center of the street. "Found Bruce Lee," he announced. "Or rather, where he will be soon."

"Really?" Georgia said surprised that all this had paid off. Or had it? "Are you sure? Will he really be there?"

"Actually, he's there," Jon pointed to the next brothel. "Presumably he's selling his fake Viagra. The police came, so he stepped into one of the houses. This guy saw him. All we have to do now is wait for him to reappear." He shepherded them down the street away from the brothels, back to the dark corner of the 'ladyboys.'

"Uh," Georgia started to protest. "Let's keep out of the bushes. Strange men are lurking there. Ladyboys," she said to Jon in way of explanation.

"The doorman confirmed what I found out about the medical certificates," Jon said, "and why they don't want you two around. The police come by at least once a night. Most of the time, they just stroll by, but occasionally they check. Tonight, just a stroll, no checks. And what is this about ladyboys on this corner? The doorman did say something. There aren't any legal gay brothels, so I guess this place has to do." He looked around the nearly deserted street intersection. "Ah, there he is," Jon said, nodding towards a young man sitting on a stool tucked just inside the gate to one of the brothels with the lights out. "The lookout. He'll call everyone if he spots the police. What a life, huh?"

They stood quietly, away from the brothels and not close enough to the bushes to be bothered.

Suddenly, Jon laughed. "Mom, you look like an angel, blonde and with a glowing halo. The rain did a number on your hair!"

Barbie reached up to touch her hair, trying to tame it by running a finger comb through it. She looked up at Jon. "Hey buddy, you have a little bit of the halo too," she remarked as she gave his hair a rake through.

"The Singapore climate does that," Georgia remarked. "Even my straighter-than-straight hair can go wild when it rains." Georgia looked up the street. "Oh, I think that's him."

Barbie looked and saw a short man swaggering up the street. He balanced himself on the balls of his feet and looked around as he headed for them. Dressed all in black, he seemed to fit into the bizarre ambiance of the place. She saw an impish smile on his face. She was not a martial arts fan; but everyone, everyone knew Bruce Lee. And this was his doppelganger.

He walked up to Jon and extended his hand, "You have been looking for me?" he asked in a thick accent.

Jon hesitated for a split second and then reached out his own hand. Barbie noticed the tenseness in this greeting, as if two sparring partners were meeting for the first time. She knew that both were into martial arts, and this casual-sounding, but potentially important meeting was drawing out the combativeness in both. Jon was younger and taller, but Bruce Lee was hard, disciplined and experienced. Jon took his hand gently and with exaggerated friendliness. "Good to finally meet you!" Jon said. "Let's talk. Where can we talk? Here?" Jon looked around, trying to find a suitable place for a conference.

"Wait, wait," Bruce Lee said, as he looked at a spot further down the street, raised his hand and produced a piercing whistle. Headlights blinked and then a taxi glided down the street, stopping directly in front of them.

"We are looking for Matt, Georgia's friend. Yannis told me that you might know where he is," Jon spoke quickly, sensing that he was about to lose Bruce Lee, the man they had been looking for all evening.

Bruce Lee looked at him. Barbie could see the inscrutable expression on his face.

"Sorry man, I don't know anything. I can't help you," Bruce said, smiling suddenly. "But would you like a ride? I'm going into the City Center. I could let you off anywhere you want."

The three sleuths looked at each other. A dead end, and now they were stuck out in the Geylang red-light district. But here was a godsend, even if it wasn't information about the missing Matt.

"Sure," Jon said, looking at the two women for confirmation.

"Might as well," Georgia said.

Bruce Lee jumped into the front seat, letting the three crowd into the back. As they smoothly pulled away from the street corner, Georgia leaned forward. "We hoped you could tell us something more about Matt, where he might have gone."

Bruce Lee, not turning around, said, "Sorry, sorry. I don't know anything."

Georgia leaned over and whispered to Barbie. "Second time tonight I've heard that 'sorry, sorry' lame excuse. I'm getting tired of that. This is wasting my time and energy. I'm just tired."

Jon leaned forward and engaged Bruce Lee in conversation, about martial arts, dojos around town, guy talk. Barbie listened with half an ear and nursed the same grudge as Georgia.

"…a number of fight clubs in that neighborhood. I have business, then I go to the clubs. I'm a celebrity!" Bruce Lee laughed merrily at his own joke. Jon laughed with him and the two conversed all the way into the city.

Suddenly Bruce Lee had a quick conversation with the driver in Chinese and soon they were pulling over. Bruce Lee jumped out and said through the open door. "He'll take you anywhere you want to go. No charge. Goodbye!" He slammed the door and walked off into the dark night.

"Where?" the driver asked the three in the back seat, looking in the rear-view mirror to catch their eyes.

Georgia looked out the window and turned to see where they had stopped. Barbie felt as though she had been on this street, maybe yesterday? But Georgia sat up with recognition and decision. "Raffles, take us to Raffles Hotel."

The driver mumbled something and again looked in the mirror, dark eyes boring into Barbie's. She tried hard to erase any expression from her face, but feared she would be unable to do so. Because she recognized the man. The fat man in the driver's seat was the owner of the bookstore in the Bras Basah Center. He too, attempted to give out no emotion, but his eyes seared a cautionary warning into her head.

Chapter Twenty-Three: Raffles Again

Barbie opened her mouth to say something, then glanced at Georgia. Georgia's body language indicated that she was in command of the situation and that Barbie needed to let Georgia handle this. Barbie felt that Georgia also recognized the driver and that the request to go to Raffles was an attempt to find a very safe place. She knew that Georgia had recognized the environs, even though Barbie wasn't sure. Within two minutes, they were pulling into one of the circular drives at the iconic hotel.

As the last to get out, Georgia proffered a $10 note to the driver. He waved her away, but it gave Georgia the chance to confirm his identity. He screeched away from the curb, ignoring the young couple standing there waiting for a taxi.

Barbie and Jon had waited at the curb while Georgia dealt with the driver. When Georgia retreated, she pulled both of them with her, deep into the interior of the hotel grounds. When they had reached a dark corner, Georgia stopped, looked around and then motioned them to gather round. "I recognized the driver," she said.

Barbie said, "So did I."

Jon nodded in agreement.

"He let Bruce Lee off in the middle of the block, and off he took. Bruce Lee was headed straight for the Bras Basah Center. I know it, I just know it."

"So why did you get the driver to bring us here?" Barbie asked.

"The Bras Basah Center is directly across the street on the west side of North Bridge Road, remember?" Georgia whispered. "We can wait just a few minutes, then we can walk out the other entrance. I had the driver bring us here to fool him. I hope it works."

"Why should we go back to the Bras Basah Center? What's there?" Jon asked.

"Something important is there. Maybe Matt's there," Georgia answered.

"You noticed that Bruce Lee told you nothing about Matt and where he went or where he might be," Barbie countered.

"Yes, I noticed that no information came out of his mouth, but his body language was different," Georgia said.

Jon chimed in the discussion. "Why don't I call Yannis? Maybe he knows something."

Barbie quickly shot back, "Do you trust Yannis?"

Both Jon and Georgia waffled.

"Yessssss," came Georgia's hesitant reply.

"I guess so," Jon mumbled.

"There's your answer, you don't trust him. You hesitated. You have your doubts," said Barbie. "So where are we going? To Bras Basah? Looking for Matt?"

Both Georgia and Jon wavered, cowed by Barbie's insightful questions.

"Where will you go there? You went yesterday. You said, Georgia, that you were going to ask this one and that one, but in the end, you asked no one. What makes you think that now, all of a sudden, you will find Matt? Where? Standing in front of the bookstore??"

Georgia stood rocking from one foot to the other as Barbie asked hard questions. She clenched her fists and made a face. "Barbie, why do you have to think so logically?"

"Because you refuse to!" came the reply.

"Ladies, ladies, no squabbling, please. This is not the time for emotions. What should we do next?" Jon stepped in.

"We need to go to Bras Basah. Bruce Lee went there. I'm positive of that. He was let off just half a block from there, although not right in front, maybe trying to throw us off. That is where it all is," Georgia tried to keep the frustration out of her voice.

"I'm not sure Bruce Lee is just hanging around Bras Basah Center, waiting to be approached by us. If he didn't answer our questions before, what makes you think he will now?" Barbie said in what she hoped was a reasonable voice.

"We could call, you have the number, don't you?" Georgia asked Barbie.

"And say what?" Jon butted in. "You didn't answer our questions about Matt when we talked last, so how about doing it now? By the way, where are you?"

Georgia peeked through some foliage behind them. "How about a very expensive coke?" she asked her companions.

"Beer?" Jon asked.

"No beer," Barbie said. "You need to keep your wits about you. Alcohol and good judgment do not go together!"

"Look! There's a quiet table over there," she pointed through the thick green leaves of a plant that separated the deserted walkway they were on from a courtyard bar.

They wended their way through several passageways, many shaded and secluded, in search of the bar they could see from the walkway near the entrance. Georgia mumbled her displeasure as they took wrong turnings and turned around on themselves. They arrived at the open-air bar just as the last group at one of the tables left. The waiter came to the secluded table as soon as they were seated. He handed them a small drinks menu.

"Mineral water, sparkling," Georgia ordered without looking.

"The same," said Barbie.

"Tiger beer, small," ordered Jon.

Barbie looked at Jon and was about to hiss at him.

"Hey, Mom, cool it!" Jon said quietly. "I can take care of myself." He turned to the waiter, "Actually, change that to soy milk." He smiled at Barbie, "Satisfied now?"

Barbie laughed and shook her head. Always joking Jon.

"But the drinks here are mighty expensive. They cost as much as three dinners elsewhere," Georgia said as she looked to make sure no one else was around. "Back to what we will do now. I'll check my phone to see if I might have missed Matt's call."

Georgia pulled her phone out of the pocket of her pack. She checked to see if there had been any calls. "Nothing new," she mumbled. "It's there. The answer is there." Georgia said more to herself than to her companions. "We went there. We wandered around. We went to the calligraphy store, the book store and looked at some of the other stores. Which one or ones were important?"

"But why didn't you ask? We went there and you didn't ask," Barbie countered.

"I didn't know what to ask. How could I ask about Matt? I didn't know who I could ask," Georgia said distractedly.

"And now you know better?" Jon asked.

"Yes! I need to ask about the drugs or the gold, or both."

Barbie piped up, "But what specifically would you ask? And who?"

Georgia ignored this and continued with her 'out-loud' thinking exercise. She leaned forward and said in a loud whisper, "The Haw Par Villa, the Chinese antiquities, the sign of 'jin'."

"But," Barbie intervened, "we went to the Haw Par Villa, we looked at the sign of 'jin' and we didn't find anything there."

"The key is in Bras Basah. The Haw Par Villa, the sign of 'jin'. Maybe they are two different clues. Not the sign of 'jin' at the Villa, but something else. Remember I said that part of the phone call was garbled? Maybe I missed part of the message?" Georgia became more and more excited as she tried to put together the clues.

Their drinks came and for a few minutes they slurped the liquid they needed after the excitement in Geylang.

"If you come with me now, I will ask this time. No more shrinking violet. I really need you guys with me. Moral support if nothing else. Last chance. I like Matt, I really do. But we've been on this for two days. Two days I have given to what?" Georgia said dejectedly.

"Are you sure?" Barbie asked.

"Yes. He needs to call me properly, or not at all." Georgia answered.

"Are you breaking up with him?" Barbie pressed.

"I don't think I have ever been 'with' him. You can't break up if you have never coupled." Georgia looked at Barbie, "I mean, well, not a proper relationship. You know what I mean."

Barbie looked quizzical, not knowing how to answer. She looked at Jon, "Is that true, Oh modern man?"

"Don't ask me. I get along with all my old girlfriends. I never 'broke up' with them, we just drifted along, apart. And my friends… We are all too young, we don't know how to break up. You tell me!" Jon sighed.

"Young? Too young? By your age, I was a bride, a mother, a divorcee and a single mother with a kid contemplating kindergarten." Barbie looked at Jon. "You young people. No backbone, no stamina, no maturity."

"You call getting married because you were pregnant a sign of maturity?" Jon countered.

"Choices is what I call it. Being able to make choices." Barbie bared her teeth at Jon.

Georgia said, "Wait a minute, this is my problem we are trying to solve here. Break up or not? This has gone on too long. I'm tired, I want my bed. I will give this one last shot."

Barbie and Jon turned to Georgia. "Good!" "Good choice."

"I'll ask a few questions, I really will. And if I get no answers, then 'poof'. End of story. No more chasing missing persons, no more phone calls to dubious friends. The end. Is that a deal?" Georgia said with a hint of triumph.

Barbie and Jon smiled and shook their heads in affirmation. The end was near.

Chapter Twenty-Four: A Return Visit to Bras
Basah

Barbie paid for the drinks and looked at the dwindling number of bills in her wallet. But it's been a wild ride. Pricey, but very interesting. Rehydrated, rested and with a plan in hand, she felt up to this one last adventure.

After a quick trip to the facilities, on the advice of Georgia that Raffles had better toilets than they would find at Bras Basah, they nimbly crossed the street to the shopping center. Barbie immediately thought that coming here now was a misguided idea. The ground floor bookstore was dark, a canvas pulled tightly over the display of books that was in front of the store. A small bulb illuminated the interior. Georgia walked up to the door and peered inside, Barbie close behind her. They could see nothing moving. A bookstore, closed for the night.

Georgia motioned to enter the main part of the complex. No one said anything, on the assumption that the only talking needed for the end of the episode of the missing boyfriend were a few questions from Georgia. The other shops were similarly closed up for the night. Lights burned inside most shops. Was it the light that dispels the darkness and harbors evil thoughts and deeds? The escalator was silent, its narrow flight of wooden slats still. The steps in repose were higher than normal stair steps and they all had difficulty negotiating them quietly.

At the top of the first flight of stairs, they watched as the night manager shooed the last of the clerks out of the big bookstore. The three young clerks headed towards the back of the building, as the man inside the store locked the door from the inside. They watched as lights went off inside.

"We've come too late, too late to catch anyone," Barbie complained.

"Yeah," Georgia conceded. "I hadn't counted on that. I'm not out this late very often. Let's go check at the calligraphy store. At least I know these people, and they might open for me if they are still there. I must be their favorite ang mo."

They dashed towards the calligraphy store, even as other lights blinked out in the far reaches of the complex. At the calligraphy goods store, a light burned in the back of the store, behind a curtain. Movements could be seen.

Georgia pounded on the closed door, and shouted. She used her hands to create a cup to block out any light from the open corridor. "There's someone there, for sure. Let me in!" she shouted again. No sound or other movement could be seen.

"Maybe they're counting money or something and don't want to answer the door for anyone," Barbie stated.

"You know that lots of people do their books the last thing in the day. They obviously don't want to be disturbed. Or maybe they're having their supper!" Jon said. "Small business owners have it hard."

"Okay, okay. Here's the thing. The bookstore is closed, although the owner just drove us in a taxi back from the red-light district. That was weird. Anyway, his bookstore is closed. The calligraphy store is closed, at least to me. That leaves one more place, the gold store, or more properly, the antiquities store. The one with the 'jin' sign. It's this way, I think." Georgia struck out confidently towards the back of the complex. Barbie and Jon trailed along.

After they had reached the farthest corner, Georgia stopped. "I'm lost, I thought it was right here, or sort of here." She looked around the immediate vicinity, a puzzled expression crinkling her face. Barbie looked around too, and felt the same disorientation. None of the shops looked familiar, as if they had wandered into the wrong shopping center.

Jon stepped forward, "Listen, I'll go this way," he pointed to the right, "and you two, stick together. Go this way, or, even better, stay right here. I'm sure it makes a loop and I'll meet you back here in two minutes. If I find the place, I'll still just come back here. Deal?"

Georgia and Barbie nodded, not knowing what else to do. Barbie suddenly felt immensely tired. Jet lag hadn't bothered her, but now, she checked the urge to consult her watch and figure out what time it was in Ankara. Only a few more minutes, and she could be out of here and heading back to Georgia's apartment and a soft, comfortable bed.

"Oh," Georgia said softly, pushing Barbie back towards the shadows. "Don't let him see us."

"Who? Why?" Barbie asked just as softly. All the same, she allowed Georgia to thrust her behind a large square pillar.

The two women watched as a guard, armed with a stick but no other observable weapons, walked quietly but firmly through the open space by the stopped escalators.

"I don't want to be asked to leave or 'escorted out'. I want to leave in my own time," she said. When he had disappeared towards the front of the complex, Georgia pulled Barbie out of the shadows.

"Damn," Georgia exclaimed. "Now I know why nothing looks familiar, it was that section, around the back of the bookstore. Remember? Not here. C'mon. We'll find that place."

"But what about Jon? He said he'd meet us here," Barbie protested.

"Oh, he'll find us. He'll remember as well. And if we don't find him, then I'll call," Georgia dragged Barbie towards the escalator.

By now, there seemed to be extremely few people around. Some stores looked as though the owners may have still been inside, like the calligraphy store, but most were dark and deserted. The few patrons of the late-night establishments had gone home. They moved slowly, creeping again towards the back side, away from North Bridge Street and the brightly lit exterior of Raffles Hotel. At one point, they came to the same large central block of small shops where they had stopped before.

Barbie whispered to Georgia. "Where's Jon? Maybe you should call him and tell him where we are."

"Let's find this place, the gold shop, and then I'll call him. He's around here somewhere, he hasn't disappeared." Georgia looked around confidently and then strode forward, taking the left-hand loop.

Then they heard it. A loud 'pop'. Just one. And because it wasn't too loud, nor repeated, it would have been easy to ignore. A car backfiring. An illegal firecracker.

"What was that?" Georgia asked.

"A gun shot," Barbie answered.

"Nooooo, couldn't be," Georgia said, her voice beginning to quaver.

"You asked. That's what it sounded like. I was being honest."

They stood still, waiting for a repeat of the noise, or a reaction, some commotion, something. Silence descended on the Bras Basah Center.

"One minute," Barbie said. "Then we move." She checked her watch and exactly one minute later, she led Georgia out of the shadows and towards the noise, which she determined came from the direction where they were headed.

As they crept silently through the wide corridors, Barbie kept on high alert. They reached the furthest most section and came to a waist high balcony railing. Over the edge, they could make out dim street lights, but no traffic.

"We're getting closer, but I think we need to go this way," Georgia whispered to Barbie as she indicated another corridor that doubled back the way they had come. As they walked quietly, Barbie suddenly recognized a few of the antique shops. Then they were there.

The shop front was as Barbie remembered it. The sign with the large 'jin' was in the window, just as it had been the day before. She thought that a lot had gone on since then. They approached the store and peered into the windows. As in some of the other stores, a light burned in the back of the shop.

"I'm calling Jon. He should be here before I knock and ask. I think I'd like to have a man around, a big man." Georgia pulled out her phone and found his number on her contact list. She pressed it.

They waited as Barbie pressed her ear to the slim crack in the front door. "I think I hear music inside," she said.

Georgia pulled the phone away from her ear and pressed her ear to the door crack as well, all the while, paying attention to the ringing of Jon's phone.

The curtains in the back of the store parted. Both women jumped back in an instinctive response to not wanting to be seen eavesdropping. "Hello, hello," called out Barbie.

Georgia did not participate in the greeting, still monitoring her phone call, but she did look up as a figure approached the door. Just as the figure reached the front of the shop, light fell on his face.

Barbie gasped and tried to move back from the door, but felt a large presence behind her. She could feel the heat and smell the body odor. Barbie looked over her shoulder and saw that the bookstore owner/taxi driver had blocked their retreat from the shop. The door opened and both women were pushed inside by the man's bulk.

"Mr. Wu, Teacher Wu," Georgia croaked, catching sight of her calligraphy teacher.

The door closed behind them as they all moved further into the interior.

"Please do come in," Mr. Wu replied. "Come this way." It was a request that would brook no refusals.

Mr. Wu turned and held back the curtain to the back room of the shop. Ghostly antiquities looked down at them as they followed the calligraphy teacher into an even smaller space. Here it was crowded with dusty old vases, jars of medicine, statuettes of ancient Chinese gods and goddesses along with rolls of calligraphy and glass cases of small objects.

Barbie hardly noticed the antiques because in front of her was her son, Jon. He sat in a chair, ropes around his ankles, his arms twisted behind his back. Silver tape covered his mouth, but his eyes spoke to her. Fear, consternation, confusion, defiance. Her heart pounded harder and harder the longer she looked at him. At a gasp from Georgia, she looked down at the floor.

In the middle of the space lay a figure sprawled on the floor, one arm tucked under him, the other thrown out to the side, as if he tried to break his fall to the cement floor. His face was recognizable. It was Bruce Lee.

A pool of dark red liquid, the same color as a good pinot noir but more viscous, spread slowly from under his head. He did not move or make any sound.

Mr. Wu joined another figure who stood opposite Barbie and Georgia. Although her tongue was frozen into muteness, she knew him. Barbie had last seen him at the ATM in the Haw Par Villa train station. Barbie stared for a long moment and then she whispered, "You."

The old man, now much more vigorous looking than he had when he wore a gardening uniform, only smiled in reply. But he held something in his hand that Barbie could not ignore and would not soon forget.

The last time Barbie faced the barrel of a gun, it was a fake plastic one, albeit a very good fake. This time she knew the gun was real. And the barrel pointed directly at her. As she watched, the black hole moved higher and closer until all she could see was the deep end of the muzzle of the gun. It was the gun that they had heard just minutes before. It was the gun that had shot someone who now lay at their feet, bleeding his way to certain death.

Her fear went beyond anything she had felt before. Great waves of terror engulfed her. Her breath, which had been held, now came quickly, erratically, in tiny shallow gulps.

"Mum," Jon said behind his shiny metal mask of tape, as he strained in his chair.

Barbie jerked into consciousness by the sound of her baby in danger. Not now. You need to keep your wits about you. You are all in danger here, fainting is not the answer. Wake up, think.

She looked once more into the small round circle that represented the blackness of oblivion.

Chapter Twenty-Five: The Gold Shop

Barbie and Georgia were silent. The men who stood around them were silent. Jon, too, had become silent. And of course, the man on the floor was silent.

Barbie tried desperately to think about the situation. Who were these men? Why did the gardener have a gun? Why had they taken Jon prisoner? Why had Bruce Lee been shot? What was Mr. Wu, the calligraphy teacher, doing here? If the gun-wielder was unstable or challenged, he might shoot them all. Careful, careful.

She knew that she needed to do all she could to preserve her life, her son's life and the life of her friend. Whatever she could do, she needed to do it soon. But she also needed a plan. She understood little of what had gone on in the past two days. At first, it all seemed like a joke, Georgia's boyfriend had gone missing. But now, the man lying on the floor, that she had seen alive less than an hour ago, was dead, or at least dying. It was not a joke.

Georgia stood next to Barbie, shaking with terror. She probably did not expect this. She probably thought it was like a comic novel, running all over Chinatown and the red-light district, meeting men in the park, taking mysterious phone calls. But now, there was the blood and the gun. What was happening here?

They heard the front door close, and then the lock snap.

"Mr. Wu, Teacher Wu," said Georgia with a quaver in her voice. "I don't understand. What... Bruce Lee..."

Mr. Wu spoke slowly, "I think you know too much, but understand too little. You need to tell us where the goods are."

Georgia licked her lips and then gnawed at them.

Mr. Wu came closer, stared at Georgia and lowered his voice. The question came out with the rumble of an angry bee. "Where are the goods?"

Georgia's courage failed. "At the sign of the 'jin'. That's all I know. Believe me, I know nothing else." Her breath came shallowly and in small noisy puffs.

The gun-wielder smiled, "Oh, you do know more, but maybe you are unaware of it."

Georgia forced herself to ask, "Why is Bruce Lee...? Is he dead? Did you shoot him?"

The man with the gun was silent. Barbie noticed that instead of the gardener's overalls, he was now dressed as a Chinese gentleman, like an old-fashioned calligrapher, like Mr. Wu. He wore loose-fitting gray trousers, a lighter gray shirt with a Mandarin collar with small frog closures. It was so contrary to the outfit that he had sported at the Haw Par Villa. Barbie was surprised that she had recognized him. But it was the eyes that had given him away. Dark coals that peered out, unblinking and totally fearless.

"I shot him," the unnamed man said. "He was a traitor."

"Xiao Lu," said Mr. Wu, "we don't need to justify anything to these people."

Xiao Lu replied calmly, "We need to make sure that they understand the seriousness of the situation." The man's sibilants issued from his mouth like the hiss of a snake that has been rudely prodded.

Georgia answered quickly, "We understand."

Barbie was silent, trying to take in all the relationships and ramifications of what was being said, by whom, and to whom. Georgia prodded her to answer. "Oh, I understand," Barbie said with no inflection.

"Good, because we need you to go to the Haw Par Villa and retrieve the goods," said Xiao Lu.

"But I don't know where they are!" Georgia protested, her voice rising to a squeak.

A hand smacked down on a counter top, causing the small glass trinkets on the counter to rattle alarmingly. "Mistake!" Xiao Lu growled.

Georgia now looked at the gun barrel which had rotated from Barbie to her. "I don't," she whimpered.

"You know, you were there. You know where they are," came the answer to her cry.

"I thought I knew. I looked, but there was nothing there!" Georgia protested.

"You lie!" retorted Xiao Lu. The gun came closer and Georgia moved back away from it as far as she could.

"I thought I knew, but I didn't. I didn't find anything." Georgia voice had fallen to a whisper.

The gun swiveled to point at Jon. He looked up at Xiao Lu with the inscrutability of a martial artist planning his next move.

Barbie concentrated on her son. How could Jon, so large, so young, so athletic, so in shape, so knowledgeable about the martial arts, ever allow himself to be caught and tied up like a wild bird? How had this happened? Then she looked at the gun and allowed her eyes to travel downward at the figure on the floor. If he had been here to see the shooting, or arrived soon after, he would have had a great deal of respect, if not fear, of the gunman, Xiao Lu. And that was another thing that Jon was, intelligent.

Xiao Lu and now smiled at Barbie. Insincere.

"Your son, I believe?" he asked.

Barbie nodded and whispered, "Yes."

"Then you need to persuade your friend to tell us all she knows," Xiao Lu said with honey dripping from his words. "Otherwise, your son will soon be like Bruce Lee, with a hole in his body and bleeding out his life."

They all looked at the floor, where the dark red pool continued to spread, but slower now. The light was not good, but Barbie did notice that Bruce Lee's face was a very pale ivory, the color drained from it.

"I will tell you," Barbie said. "I looked, we all looked, but we found nothing. I am telling the truth. There was nothing there. You cannot hurt my son for nothing."

Xiao Lu laughed, a strained maniacal laugh that Barbie recognized as madness, with a tinge of fear. She understood that Xiao Lu may not only be evil, but mad as well.

"Tell me. Tell me or you will all die!" Xiao Lu snarled.

Mr. Wu put a hand on Xiao Lu's arm. "Not yet, all in good time." He turned to Georgia. "It's better that you tell us everything you know, everything."

Barbie turned to Georgia. "Tell him. There's nothing to tell anyway." Barbie hoped that she was conveying to Georgia to reveal as little as she could get away with. Mr. Wu and friend already knew that the three of them had been to the Haw Par Villa, presumably looking for something. And Georgia had let slip the 'sign of the jin' bit, so what more could they say? Lots, but maybe they needed to keep some things back as bargaining chips. "You remember, Georgia, the anonymous phone call, from someone? They said, Haw Par Villa, sign of the 'jin' and nothing else, remember?" She elbowed Georgia, who had gone very pale and still. "Georgia, tell them."

"Yeah," Georgia answered, "that's right. I had no idea where the call was from, no number on my phone."

"Was it from your friend Matt? It must have been, who else would send you to Haw Par Villa?" Xiao Lu demanded.

"I thought it was, but the voice, wasn't, well, wasn't clear," Georgia stumbled, trying to catch Barbie's eye.

"She thought at first it was," Barbie answered for her, "but later she thought maybe it wasn't. Maybe it was someone pretending to be Matt. She kept asking who it was and he, if it was a he, didn't answer, just static, right Georgia?"

Georgia nodded miserably. "That's all I know," she whispered.

"Give me your phone!" demanded Xiao Lu.

Georgia handed him her small backpack. "It's in the inside pocket." She shook as she held out the black pack.

Barbie felt very uncomfortable. What was Georgia thinking about, handing over her phone? Who had she called? What numbers were on there? I remember that I took down the numbers in my notebook, but Georgia had refused to call any of them. Jon was the one who had called Yannis.

Yannis! Where was Yannis? He seems to be the only one who hasn't been around lately. Jon saw him this morning, and Yannis told him where to find Bruce Lee, the dead Bruce Lee, and then didn't show up in Geylang to meet them as promised. What had happened to Yannis?

Mr. Wu had received the pack from Georgia, as Xiao Lu was busy holding a gun on the two women. He placed it on a narrow shelf, hastily cleared of antiquities. Xiao Lu barked, "Open it, find the phone!"

Mr. Wu reached out a hand and touched the opening, a black gaping hole. He jerked his hand away. "This is a private place, a woman's private place."

Barbie had visions of the backpack as a metaphor for a woman's… No, do not go there. Do not laugh at Mr. Wu. Should I offer to do it for him? To save him from violating a woman?

"Let the other one do it," Mr. Wu said.

Barbie found her mouth opening. "I'll do it, I'll take it out."

"No," screamed Xiao Lu. "Where is the young man?"

Mr. Wu's head jerked towards the back of the room, where a thin black cloth hid a back door.

"Come, come here," shouted Xiao Lu at the barely concealed door.

A noise came from the lock, as the knob twisted and the door creaked open. In answer to her silent question, Yannis pulled the thin cloth aside and stepped out of the shadows. A smile lit his face as he came into the crowded space.

Chapter Twenty-Six: Plans for the Return to Haw Par Villa

Barbie's mouth fell open. It was as if she had summoned him by thinking of him.

Georgia whispered, "Yannis."

Trying not to let anyone else hear, Barbie whispered to Georgia, "You said you trusted him!"

"I trusted him," she answered. "How could he do… this??"

A noise behind them caused Barbie to turn to the front of the store. A looming figure blocked out any light from the corridor outside. It was the Evernew book store owner, aka the taxi driver. Oh my god, four men against two women, and our only ally is tied up! She felt her knees buckle beneath her and before she could catch herself, she slid to the floor, causing a wooden box to fall. It broke open with a 'crash' and spilled its contents on the floor next to Barbie. She saw a miniature Buddha, its cheap gold paint glinting in the feeble light. "Sorry," she mumbled.

"You will go again to the Haw Par Villa. You will find the treasure. We, too, have heard from our sources. It has been delivered today. The same methods that have been used in the past. But today, there is a different place," Xiao Lu declared, looking down at the dead body of Bruce Lee. "We need to find that place."

"But we looked," Georgia stammered. She turned to Barbie, who was now trying to lift herself up from the inelegant position on the floor. She offered her hand and pulled Barbie up. "Didn't we? We looked at the sign of the 'jin'."

"It must be a different place. You will find it," Xiao Lu reiterated. "You will be accompanied. Both of you will go, I have a hostage, which means you will be cooperative." He laughed the hollow laugh of the desperate. He had been speaking to Georgia, but now his eyes swiveled and bored into Barbie's. "You will do nothing except what I tell you. If you try anything… I will use this on your son…" He jiggled the gun in Jon's direction.

"He was arrogant," Xiao Lu said, kicking the inert body of Bruce Lee. "He thought he could do anything based on his resemblance to a famous person. He thought this physical similarity would protect him. He thought it made him special. 'Bruce Lee' he called himself, but he was just another street boy. Like all the others, as soon as they get their fix, their powder, they forget. They forget where they come from. The drugs make them think they are gods, or movie stars!" He laughed again.

Barbie thought furiously. He was talking about 'powder', drugs, not fake Viagra. Maybe all this was not about the simple Chinese drugs sold on the street, but hard drugs. The delivery of the drugs was through the port of Singapore, opposite the Haw Par Villa. That's what Matt was doing there, meeting the delivery of drugs. What was Georgia thinking when she got entangled with a drug supplier? What about the fake Viagra? How did it get involved with the other drugs? Were those dealers she saw in Geylang involved in the heroin trade? Very dicey in Singapore. They give people the death penalty for that. She looked at the inert body of the 'misguided boy' on the floor. Frontier justice?

She looked at Yannis, now standing near the two women. She couldn't look him in the eye. She thought he was on their side, or at least neutral, a go-between. But this? She thought that Jon knew him better than she, and that Georgia knew him even better than Jon. But they were both wrong. How could they have been such bad judges of character?

Barbie watched as Yannis took Georgia's bag. He found the phone easily, not being afraid of violating Georgia's space, and was now scrolling through the calls. "No calls received. No calls made. No suspicious contacts. Oh, here's one, a phone call, early this afternoon. Incoming call, no number."

"What was this call?" Xiao Lu demanded of Georgia.

"I've already told you everything I know," Georgia said again, tears springing to her eyes. "He said, 'the Haw Par Villa, sign of 'jin'. Nothing more. I can't tell you something I don't know!" she said with a great sob, tears now streaming down her cheeks.

Barbie thought she was very frightened. That, or she was a superb actress.

"Take them both to the Haw Par Villa," Xiao Lu demanded. "They will find the treasure. The two of you," he jerked his head towards the fat man. "Go, now!" He waved his gun again.

Barbie looked at Jon, tied up in the chair. She saw fear in his eyes. This was her baby, her only child. She had not seen him in eight years, playing out some bizarre ritual of longing, punishment, wanting to be near him, afraid of facing him. She had cried many times for her stupidity in not spending time with him. Now he was here, so close and yet in so much danger of not being here when she came back. She looked at the dead Bruce Lee and her feelings burst out, "Jon, I'm so sorry. This is all my fault. I was trying to punish you for leaving me. I wanted you to suffer because you broke my heart. I thought you rejected me in favor of him. He's so NOT worth your love. I thought that you were being so cruel to me. That's what I thought and that's why I punished you. By being busy, by not being able to meet you. It was to punish you. But then I realized that you didn't do it to hurt me, but to find yourself. But by that time, the pattern was there. And then you started punishing me for trying to punish you! Oh, what a mess. I'm sorry Jon, I'm so very, very sorry. I love you, you are my son. My darling Jon. If…if I never see you again, if, if we both die, I want you to know how sorry I am. I want you to know that I have punished myself more by not making sure to meet you." Barbie's tears poured down her face as she spoke to Jon. She took Jon's arm in both hands as she wept. Jon's eyes filled with anguished tears.

Startled by the outburst, the others remained silent. When Barbie reached out to touch Jon's arm, Xiao Lu stepped up and thrust the gun in Barbie's face. "Back away… No nonsense. No tears. None of you will die if you do what you are told. This one," he kicked Bruce Lee's body again. "He was getting greedy."

Xiao Lu back away again, this time grinning. "Ah, now I know something important. You love your son, very much. So, you will go along. You will be good. You will make sure your friend does as she is told. You will bring me my reward." He made a garbled noise in his throat that Barbie interpreted as a chuckle, an evil chuckle.

Yannis and the fat bookstore owner now surrounded Barbie and Georgia and gently guided them out the back door. Barbie looked back as she went out, but the fat man blocked her view of Jon. She gasped at what she was afraid was the last contact with her son, denied the view of his face.

The progress through the back of the store was slow. The short passageway was dimly lit and lined with stacks of cardboard boxes, piled high. Even higher shelves held dusty curios of undetermined age or value. Yannis went first, followed by Georgia, then Barbie. The fat man squeezed in behind her as Barbie tried not to sneeze as they disturbed the dust. The man behind her wheezed and brushed up against the boxes, at one point turning sideways to move through. Eventually they came to the back door. Yannis held it open, his arm arching over them as they exited.

Barbie tried to ignore the presence of the two men as the group proceeded into the dimly lit back part of the shopping center. Yannis stood close to the two women as he herded them towards the even darker corner nearby. Yannis led them to a tiny lift in a dead-end corridor. He went in first and held the button to hold the door open. The fat man pushed his bulk into the miniscule space. Barbie tried to read the instructions to find out if the four of them were 'legal' in the small lift. She wondered if they would make it due to the weight. As they jockeyed for space, Yannis asked her, "You okay?"

Barbie tried to give him a filthy look, but had no way of twisting her neck around to face him. She mumbled a reply, then asked, "Are you sure we're going to make it?"

Jon pushed the 'B' for basement and the lift's mechanical voice groaned in reply. The lift jerked and then began a moaning descent. Barbie held her breath, hoping to lighten the load. The small box hit the basement floor and then did a knee-shattering bounce. They waited for the door to open. Yannis muttered and then reached over the women's head to the control panel. Barbie felt the heat from his body as he leaned in towards her. How dare he get so close. The traitor! His handsome face leaned to within an inch of her cheek.

The doors eventually sneezed and then clanked open. The fat bookstore owner backed out and kept close to the others as they gingerly untangled themselves. Yannis was last, but kept his eyes on the two women. The fat man led them through the dusty, moldy interior of an underground parking lot. As they wended their way through the dim place, Barbie thought of trying to escape. No, not here, not now. What about Jon?

They approached the familiar taxi and the fat man unlocked the doors. Georgia was pushed towards the front seat. Jon watched her get in and then indicated to Barbie that she should get in the back. He slid in beside her and slammed the door shut. Once again, Barbie felt the heat of his body as she shivered.

Georgia's door still stood open and Yannis jabbed at her back. "Close it!" he growled.

Georgia reached out and closed the door. The fat man settled himself in the driver's seat. Georgia trembled in the front seat. "Seat belt," the fat man demanded. Georgia ignored him.

"Buckle up your seat belt," Yannis shouted from the back seat, again poking Georgia's shoulder. "No nonsense. Do as you are told!" he demanded. "We don't want to attract any attention."

Barbie heard the slick 'snick' of the knife before she saw it. The huge blade glinted in the dim light. Yannis brought the knife up close to Georgia's head so that she could see it. Georgia turned around to glance at the threatening blade. She nodded involuntarily, then shifted her body into a forward position. At attention as it were. She reached for the seat belt and pulled it across her chest, snapping it into place.

Barbie hadn't noticed the firm grip that Yannis had inflicted on her arm, she had been so absorbed with the knife's appearance. Now, she tried to make his large powerful hand loosen so that the blood could flow to her arm. "Okay, okay," she whimpered, trying to use her fingers to pry his loose.

"We are going to the Haw Par Villa. You will do as you are told to do," Yannis spoke softly, but with uncalculated menace. "If you don't, you will end up like Bruce Lee."

Barbie closed her eyes as she felt the car swing out of the parking space. She thought of Bruce Lee on the floor of the antique shop. Tears forced themselves through her eyelids and trickled down her face.

Chapter Twenty-Seven: The Sign of 'Jin'

The streets were deserted at this late hour. The taxi had its sign off so no one would try to hail it in the quiet streets. Barbie noticed that the sidewalks appeared and disappeared in pools of lights from the streetlights, and that there were no pedestrians out. Barbie dared not look at her watch, not wanting to call attention to her nervousness, but at this hour the only neighborhoods awake would be Geylang and other places of the night. How can you hope to call attention to a kidnapping, for that's what this was, if there was no one to call out to?

The car swayed around corners, throwing Barbie against her seatbelt and Yannis' arm, the one that still held the knife. She tried to look out the window and figure out where they were. Nowhere looked like a place she had been before, but everywhere looked vaguely familiar; tall trees, lush street side vegetation, staggered street lights at regular intervals. Soon they arrived at a gate. Within seconds of arrival, the sturdy metal fence began a groaning retreat along a metal track across the road. Barbie looked for a human presence, but saw nothing. They entered and the car slowed as it wound its way up and around a narrow roadway. Barbie looked back and saw the ghostly gate close behind them.

Then the car pulled into a small empty parking lot and stopped. In the dim light, Barbie saw a massive open building in front of them; statues loomed around the outside. She recognized the style, the lifelike figures with arms upraised, poised to strike miscreants or evildoers with swords, sticks or bolts of celestial lightening. They were at the Haw Par Villa, at the pavilion on the top of the hill. Earlier they had seen the front of the building on their wanderings.

The security lights were on, but they were dim and did not penetrate the deep shadows. The driver cum bookstore owner heaved himself out of the car and slammed the door shut. Yannis opened his door and then motioned for the two women to get out. As they stood near the car, Barbie heard the noise of a snuffling dog. The deep 'snrf, snrf' made her think it was a large one, possibly the one they had encountered earlier in the day. Barbie tried to think of who she could hide behind if the dog came closer. The fat man was the obvious choice. She slid around behind him.

As they moved forward, a uniformed man moved out of the shadows, holding the snuffling dog on a leash. The hands of the security guard and the fat man met, briefly, then parted. Barbie had the impression that money had slipped between the palms, but nothing was clear in the obscurity of the deserted gardens. The uniformed man and the dog backed off, with one last 'snrf' from the hound.

Yannis grabbed the two women, one in each arm. Barbie noticed the absence of the knife, but felt it was close at hand. "The sign of 'jin'," he said, pulling them forward into the gloom.

Eerie tableaux of Chinese gods and goddesses lurked around them as they moved. At first the fat man led, but then he turned around and let Yannis and the women go ahead of him. They proceeded downhill. Barbie tried to get her bearings, tried to place herself in the maze that she had surely been in earlier in the day.

The fat man breathed heavily behind them. "Do you know this place, the sign of 'jin'?" he asked.

Georgia looked around at him, causing the small group to stumble and split apart. Yannis quickly reasserted himself by latching on to their arms again.

"The sign he asked you? Do you know?" he asked again.

"I think so," stuttered Georgia. "I think I found it this afternoon. But nothing was there," she said. "What was I looking for?"

"We will know when we get there," answered Yannis, his hand pinching harder around Barbie's arm.

Barbie squirmed under his powerful grip, causing her to miss her step. She bumped against Yannis and he growled at her. He clamped down harder and then Georgia yipped in pain. Barbie thought it would have been better to be faced with a knife, rather than this pinching and grabbing. What does Yannis think I am going to do? Run? Put that thought away, it is not just you who is in this mess. Think of your friend…and your son.

The fat man now took the lead, waddling quickly down the hill, turning the corners with confidence, leading them onwards. Soon the yawning black entrance to the Ten Courts of Hell appeared in front of them. Barbie remembered the sign in front. The interior was sinister enough in daylight, but what would it be like at night? No lights appeared within. Oh good, Courts of Hell, black winding walkways and two big men who did not wish them well.

"Lights, tell the man to turn on the damn lights," Yannis said to the hulking back in front of them.

"No problem," the fat man said, pulling out his phone. He tapped the side and a bright light spat out the front.

Yannis groaned and took out his own phone, turning on a dimmer light. The two pinpoints did not reach far. Barbie was able to make out dim shapes of the winding walkway and the fake rocks that reached out to snatch unsuspecting shins and to block views. The dim lights flashed back and forth across the figures, whose bloody knives looked even more menacing in the dim light. The red of the blood looked more real and less like paint in the murk.

They shuffled along for an indeterminate amount of time. Barbie felt they must be near the end of the tunnel, but nothing ahead looked like 'outside'. Suddenly, a rock reached up and grabbed her ankle, causing her to squeak in alarm and stumble into Yannis. A strong arm reached out and grabbed Barbie just as a growl emerged, "Watch yourself, sister!" The fat man turned around and shone his phone light directly in Barbie's eyes.

"Stop, I can't see anything," Barbie said, throwing up her arm to shade her eyes. Immediately, she felt Yannis' arm grip hers in a pincer movement. "Not so tight, I'm not going anywhere," she offered in defense. Where would I go?

Barbie let go of her anxiety then. Where would I go? Where could I go? Maybe this is the time to break free? After all, she could use her 'voice' and distract the two men, then she and Georgia might be able to make a run for it. She remembered her previous use of the ventriloquists' voice that she had learned from her father. She had been taught to throw her voice, in the guise of animals, humans, whatever; into corners, niches, behind someone or something, thus confusing and frightening her pursuers. Could she distract the fat man and Yannis long enough to get out of here? And then they could hide?

Perhaps it was worth a try. They penetrated deeper into the Courts of Hell. Now there was no ambient light from outside, and the only light was from the fat man's phone. Barbie turned her head, trying to see into the corners, the recesses. She started with a low growl. There was no reaction from the fat man or Yannis. Georgia said nothing. Barbie tried another growl, longer and louder, trying to find a distant corner to bounce the sound off.

"What was that?" Yannis asked, yanking the two women to a stop.

Barbie tried again, another growl came from the hanging rocks and jutting figures. "What was that?" Yannis demanded again.

"Dog," answered the fat man.

Barbie tried to get closer to Georgia, to whisper to tell her that it was a 'Barbie dog', not the one they had encountered earlier. She tried to find Georgia in the dark, but only managed to trip over Yannis' feet. "Quiet!" demanded Yannis.

Barbie waited, they all waited. Slowly, Barbie tried again, turning her head to try and make the 'dog' sound like it was behind them. She ended this latest growl with a 'yip'.

Yannis exploded with a string of expletives in some unknown language, maybe Greek. "I thought I told you to make sure that dog was far away! Didn't you tell him?"

The fat man hesitated. "Yes, I told him. No dog. He was paid."

Suddenly Barbie felt the heat from the fat man's body next to hers. Did he know? Or suspect? She held her breath, keeping totally silent.

"If I see that man or that dog," Yannis said menacingly.

"No, no. No dog," came the answer from the fat man.

Barbie thought better of her idea. She remembered Bruce Lee's body leaking blood onto the floor. The dog wasn't really a threat for them, but it might make them more nervous and thus more trigger happy, or Yannis more likely to use that long sharp knife. No, no, scrap that idea. Besides, even if they got away, what would happen to Jon? He might be in more jeopardy. Bad idea, Barbie.

Their progress slowed now, but the small pushes from Yannis kept the women moving forward, deeper into the Courts of Hell. Barbie looked around as the light moved slowly over the small figures in their agonies of torture. She saw the moneylenders stabbed through and slowed. Was this the sign of the 'jin'? Money? "Psst, Georgia?" Barbie whispered.

The light turned to shine on Barbie's face, but not before she had glimpsed the recognition in Georgia's eyes. Barbie nodded 'yes' and tipped her head towards the hillside of knives, just to their left.

Georgia hesitated and then stammered, "This, maybe. Here."

The light swung to illuminate the gruesome tableau. There was a platform and perched on it was an angry priest/god. Below was a hillside of knives that protruded like needles on a pincushion. The moneylenders had been chucked off the platform, landing on the knives that pierced their bodies. Copious red paint had been applied to the knives, the bodies and the hillside.

"This, here?" Yannis demanded.

"Maybe," Georgia said. "But I looked here, all around, nothing was here." Georgia pointed to the sign that detailed the punishment for moneylenders. "See, there?"

They all peered at the sign. Even the fat man grunted in frustration as they tried to find the 'jin' in among the hundred characters that told the story for the Chinese visitors.

"I'll look," the fat man mumbled as he lifted a leg and climbed over the short cement wall.

Barbie watched as the light flickered among the figures and then disappeared behind the hillside. "What are we looking for?" Barbie asked meekly.

No answer came, even though the fat man and Yannis seemed to know.

There came the sound of a bump, a mumbled curse and then a statue slowly tipped over and crashed to the floor. Barbie jumped in surprise. The noise of the plaster shattering broke the spell. Barbie expected to be surrounded by dogs and security guards any minute. Until she remembered it was she who had created the dog.

"Aha," came a shout from the dust cloud that surrounded the remaining god figures. The fat man grunted as he held up a small suitcase, shining the now dimming light on it.

Then the case fell at his feet. A second loud crash in a matter of minutes strummed at Barbie's nerves. "Hauhhhh," she uttered, trying to catch her breath.

"Heavy. Very, very heavy." The fat man bent over and struggled to regain the black suitcase.

Barbie's mind leaped into gear. The gold, the thirty kilos of gold. Could this be it? In this small suitcase, a very heavy suitcase?

Her thoughts were interrupted as Yannis, at her side, began to squeal in pleasure, "Yes, yes, yes. This is it."

Chapter Twenty-eight: The Lost Treasure

The fat man laughed. A big hearty Santa Claus ho-ho-ho that ended in a snorting chortle. Barbie thought it was not a pleasant laugh, but a giggle of glee. The light swung wildly as the man inched over the debris. The heavy bag swung at his side, banging his leg and bouncing off the small statues. He walked right over the hill of knives, crunching them under his feet like a modern-day Gulliver in a Lilliputian scene.

Carefully, he climbed over the wall and joined Yannis. "Is this it? Is this the shipment?" Yannis asked, the excitement barely suppressed in his voice.

The fat man answered with another chuckle, "Feel for yourself." He crowded closer to Yannis and held out the bag, struggling to maintain control of his emotions. He held the bag tightly.

Yannis leaned over and felt the bag, first trying to feel the contents, then slipping his hand under it and giving it a gentle lift. "Hmph! That's it. Let's go."

The fat man struck out in front, holding the small heavy bag in one hand and his phone with the light in the other. Yannis followed with the two women, one on either side, as before. They retraced their steps easily and when they emerged from the Courts of Hell, the ambient light of

Singapore seemed like daylight in comparison to the blackness of Hell.

They scurried quickly, or as quickly as it was possible, as the fat man struggled to balance the heavily weighted bag. Yannis mumbled a few times about carrying it for a while, but the fat man stumbled faster at the suggestion.

Barbie noted the distant roar of the freeway traffic. That day, the gardens had been quiet, a peaceful island in the midst of bustling Singapore. But now, it was as if they were in a world apart, isolated in a fantasy bubble. Is that really gold in the small black bag? Bars or bricks of gold stolen almost 70 years ago? Only now making its debut? If it hadn't been for the knife she knew was in the pocket of the man who gripped her arm, and the bloody mess back at the shopping center, she might have thought it a grand joke.

Soon they were at the car. Barbie's shoulders drooped at the thought that her opportunity had been squandered, and that it was too late now to make a break for it. The fat man unlocked the car, and then walked around to the back. He unlocked the trunk and with a grunt, dumped the heavy bag in the well. Barbie saw the car bounce gently with the weight just as she felt the nudge on her shoulder.

"No," Yannis said. "Inside with us, not in the trunk! The fat man, who was attempting to insert himself into the front seat, grunted in reply. He got out and retraced his journey to the trunk. Barbie saw the car bounce gently again as the weight was lifted out of the trunk. "Here, put it here, on the floor." Yannis demanded.

"But this is the goods! We have it now," the fat driver protested.

"Don't you think it will be safe here? Whose side are you on? It's safe with me." The bag was dropped onto the floor of the back seat. "Time to go," Yannis said. First, he watched Georgia get into the front seat, then he shoved at Barbie, pushing her in one door in the back and forcing her to slide across the seat. Her feet banged against the bag. She could feel the corner of something solid. Yannis got in and snuggled the bag between his feet. The knife reappeared.

The driver retraced his route down the hill. The gate opened in front of them and closed behind them as before. Barbie saw no one. The ride back to Bras Basah Center was even faster than their trip out. It was unclear whether they took the same route or not.

Barbie stared out the window, but did not absorb the scenes she saw. Her mind flitted from scenario to scenario, trying to puzzle her way out of this box. How can I escape? What can I use to defeat these evil men? In the end, she rejected all ideas. She reasoned that Jon needed to be part of the escape, and at the moment, he was still being held hostage.

The car pulled into the garage and slowly glided to an empty space near the elevator. Yannis leaped out and pulled open the front door for Georgia and motioned for Barbie to exit on his side of the car. The driver also exited quickly, slammed his door and scampered to Yannis' side. Yannis had the bag firmly in his grip and there was a tense stand-off as both men maneuvered to carry the small black suitcase.

"The lift isn't strong enough for all of us, I'll take the bag," the fat man said.

"No, we'll all climb the stairs! And I can carry this," Yannis announced as he turned and headed for the staircase, not far from the elevator.

The night air was close and warm here. The basement smelled of car exhaust, garbage and mold. Barbie tried to breathe, but gagged on each breath. Georgia stumbled as they proceeded towards the stairs. Barbie wanted to berate her for involving her in this terrible tragedy, but Barbie realized that she had gone into it with eyes open. Now it was too late to back out, to renege on promises to help find Matt.

They proceeded up the staircase in single file, the dim lights not reaching to the corners, making progress slow. Somehow or other, Barbie noticed that now the fat man carried the bag; his shuffling gait and labored breathing betrayed his struggle with the heavy weight. Does the bag really hold 30 kilos of gold? If so, it is dammed heavy. I wonder if I could even pick it up?

As they reached the second level of the building, the night air rushed to greet them. Barbie sucked in a large breath and felt better. Before she realized it, they stood before the store. The curtains in front were tightly closed and a cursory look would have revealed nothing amiss. But Barbie knew there were people inside and she could see the dim lights that faded and wavered with the movement of people.

Yannis knocked. All movement stopped and then Barbie could see the outline of someone moving the curtain in the back and coming through the store. They stood together at the front door, in the lights of the center, clearly illumined for anyone inside to see. Mr. Wu cautiously opened the door.

No words greeted their entry. They filed into the front room and proceeded to the back room, the curtain swinging closed behind them. The lights had been dimmed, but nothing had been moved. The body lay on the floor; Jon was strapped into the chair. The fat man lifted the black bag and allowed a wide smile to cross his face.

Mr. Wu started the conversation. Rapid Chinese whirled among the three Chinese speakers. Barbie didn't know any Chinese, but she did know body language. It was obvious that Mr. Wu was in charge. He berated the fat man, who attempted to rebut Mr. Wu.

Soon, the bag was placed gingerly on the countertop nearest Xiao Lu. The fat man turned and went out. Barbie heard the front door open and close. Through the slit in the side of the curtain, she saw his broad back in the doorway. He looked right and left, his legs spread to a fighting stance. The guard at the door.

Yannis moved over closer to the bag, which Barbie saw distinctly for the first time. It was a small duffle-type bag, rounded on top, with a reinforced flat bottom. It looked much too small to hold anything that weighed 30 kilos, except lead. Or gold.

Xiao Lu took hold of the handles possessively and gently lifted the bag. Barbie realized by the way he moved his body that he, too, must be a martial artist. Slender, fit, with the grace of a large cat, he gently moved the handles back and slowly unzipped the bag. He turned to Georgia and Barbie, who had remained silent.

"Thank you for rescuing this. You do know what it is, don't you?" Xiao Lu gave them a shark's grin.

Georgia, her eyes fixated on the bag, blurted out. "Thirty kilos of gold. It was lost many years ago in the Himalayas. The payment for a double-cross. And now it is here."

"That is one story. But this was not lost. It was stolen, stolen from my people by the capitalist running dogs. It was taken from its rightful owners." Xiao Lu spoke with passionate vehemence.

"How do you know this?" Barbie asked. "I thought it was lost. At least that's what the book said."

"My child, you are so naïve. You have been educated in a country that was founded by naïve creatures, who thought the very best of human nature. Lost? I am a scholar, a scholar of history. MY history. I have been looking for this all of my life. Not lost, but stolen. But now, it will fund the resurgence. That is my dream, from the first moment I knew about this treasure. This will save my people, and my country."

Barbie could almost see his eyes glow with fanaticism. It was an eerie performance, and he held center stage.

"Eight hundred lan of gold," he continued. "Some may be missing, there was sure to be a few lan that went to those who carried it so far. I cannot begrudge that. The treasure has finally come to me. It has found the right courier, at last. Now we shall see. Now we shall all see."

Xiao Lu unzipped the bag. Barbie smelled the sea, the mold of ships' holds. She craned her neck to see into the depths of the black hold-all.

Xiao Lu reached his hand inside and closed it around something. He pulled his hand out and a handful of Styrofoam peanuts fell from between his fingers to the floor. They all watched as he reached his hand in again. This time it emerged with a cloth bag that clanked.

He took a breath of anticipation as he put the bag on the glass-topped counter. The bag was tied shut, and then a drawstring had been used to close it tighter. In any case, Xiao

Lu struggled to get it open and ripped the bag with a dull 'scritch'. Three dark oblong bars toppled over on the counter. He reached for the topmost one and cradled it in his hand. Black dust or soot came off on his palms. He reached for the bag and used it to rub the black dust off the object until the shimmer of gold came through. He laughed.

He continued to grin as he reached for the other bars and started to rub them as well. Mr. Wu said something in Chinese, which caused Xiao Lu to stop. "No, it can't be. It can't be paint. Look! Look at this!" Xiao Lu exposed the bar to the brightest light in the room, directly over Bruce Lee's body.

Barbie was not close enough to judge definitively, but she saw gold color, although a little too bright perhaps. Just then Xiao Lu snatched it out of the light, while he fumbled for the other two bars of gold.

"No, no," he screeched, reaching for a knife. He scraped at the outside of one of the bars. Soon, gold bits flaked and fell to the floor. Underneath the gold was another layer, this one of dull lead gray. "No, they have cheated me!" He hacked some more on another part of the gold ingot, revealing more dull gray underneath the gold paint. He grabbed another one and hacked some more. "It's fake. Lead painted gold. We've been cheated."

"You," Xiao Lu looked down at Bruce Lee's body. "You are a liar and a cheat. Why did you do this? You double-crossed me. Where is the gold?"

Mr. Wu, with a puzzled look, tried to restrain the other man from kicking the body again. "Why do you think it was he who double-crossed you? Maybe it was someone else?" He jerked his head towards the door.

Xiao Lu looked at the door, then at the useless bar in his hand. He hurled it through the thin curtain towards the front of the building.

Barbie heard the rip of the curtain and the shattering of the glass door. Then she heard the 'oomph' of the fat man falling forward onto the gray cement floor.

Chapter Twenty-nine: Escape

Barbie waited only a second for the chaos. If the fake gold brick through the window wasn't going to do it, she was. She puckered her lips and sent out an alarm. She wasn't quite sure what sound alarms were in Singapore, every country having their own ambulance, police and fire alarm sounds, but she made a headache splitting one, right in the middle of the tiny store. She sucked in her breath after the first wild whistling sound, and tried to throw it so that it sounded like it came from outside, next door, or across the corridor.

Before she could let go with a third alarm, she felt Georgia's pull from behind her. As she was forcibly dragged back towards the back door of the shop, she pursed her lips again, this time making a whoop-whoop sound that echoed in the small space. Then the lights went out.

Barbie tried not to tread on the body on the floor, but she had no visual clues to guide her. She allowed herself to be pulled from behind, all the while filling the air with noise. She hoped it was helping their escape, not hindering it. In between her noises, she heard shouting in English and in Chinese. It was as if anger, disappointment and, finally, a reveling in revenge filled the space.

Suddenly, Barbie realized that the sounds of alarms were not all coming from her mouth. Outside there were bells like those in her elementary school during a fire alarm. Mixed in were ambulance 'whooey-whooey' sounds. She figured that the fake brick through the window may have set off alarms, as it should have done.

She turned around and now saw the back door, an open rectangle letting in some dim outside light. Against the light, she saw the silhouette of a person slipping out. She also saw the outlines of a chair; the chair that Jon had been strapped into. She reached for it, but it tumbled over onto the floor. No one was there. She reached for the arms and encountered sticky tape, obviously cut. "Jon, Jon," she whispered into the darkness. No one answered. Where has he gone? Oh, thank goodness, he's managed to get out. It must have been him slipping out the back door. But why has he abandoned me? "Jon?" she called, louder this time.

Georgia answered, "C'mon. Let's go! Out the back!"

"Did Jon get out? Was it him I saw leaving? We can't leave without him!"

In the front of the store, Barbie now heard the two older Chinese men. No attempt was made to keep their voices down as they argued with one another. More glass shattered. The sound of objects falling on the floor or being thrown came to Barbie and Georgia.

"This way," Georgia said, again pushing Barbie.

"But Jon, where is he?" Barbie said again. She hoped it was he she saw leaving.

She tripped over something and fell heavily to the floor. Soft clothes and a sticky substance met her outstretched hand. "Oh God, it's Bruce Lee. Georgia, where are you? Jon, help!"

"Mom, I'm here." Jon's soft voice came with a strong arm, helping her up. "Out, this way, now!"

The three managed to exit one after the other through the back door. When they emerged, the dim lights confused them. There was noise, lots of it, coming from the front part of the shop. Arguing in Chinese, breaking glass, thumps of things falling, and it was all mixed in with emergency sirens and alarms.

"This way," Jon demanded as they raced around the corners. Georgia headed for the lift, Barbie spied the staircase and raced for it. Jon aimed for the escalator. Suddenly, the entire shopping complex fell into darkness.

Barbie stood still, confused and frightened. "Jon, Georgia," she called. Suddenly, she felt lost, and alone.

A figure moved slowly in the murky light. "Jon," Barbie whispered.

"This way," came the answer.

A grip of steel ringed Barbie's arms, in the very same place Yannis had gripped her.

"No," she quavered, certain it was Yannis and that she had been caught.

"Yes, this way," came the answer.

Barbie froze. She couldn't go with him. She had been so close to escape, but now, recaptured. No, this wasn't right.

With his grip tightening, Barbie had no choice. She was bodily hauled towards what she was sure was the escalator. The noises in the rest of the complex swelled and died down. She guessed that most of them came from outside. But what happened to the lights? Presumably all the electricity had been doused.

Yannis shoved her onto the escalator. The Bras Basah Center had been built many years before, not the most glamourous shopping mall in Singapore. It had always been known as a cheap place to rent a shop, and most of the businesses were small, specialty shops, mostly in the field of the arts. No one was interested in upgrading the common facilities if it meant higher rents. This escalator was extraordinarily narrow and the steps were made of wooden slats. Barbie was pushed on first, while Yannis stood close behind her, still gripping her arm. The heat from his body made Barbie's already frightened mind race faster. She could smell the sweat of adrenalin as he used his body to push her forward.

The steps were high and awkward, now that they were not moving, and Barbie stumbled continuously as she tried to negotiate them. Or was she stumbling because she did not want to go with Yannis? Pinned like a moth. Pushed around like a toy doll. She reached for the steps down, trying to take her time, snatching seconds from the inevitable recapture at the bottom.

The steps beneath her feet slowly growled and came to life. They started moving with a squeal. But they were moving upwards, not down. Her journey down was now a double time one. Yannis pushed her again. "Hurry," he said softly in her ear.

The lights flickered on, then off, and then on again. They were obviously the emergency lights as shadows still lurked in the corners. Now she could hear people moving, shouting in the distance. The push from behind became even more insistent.

Being able to see was not much help and Barbie had to choose between resistance to the evil man at her back and the desire to go down, where she felt sure she would be safer. She quickened her steps down, even as the escalator gained strength and began to move faster in the opposite direction. She noticed the escalator next to them going down quickly. "We're on the wrong escalator," she whined.

"Just keep moving, make your legs go faster, go down, quickly now." Yannis grabbed both her arms and practically lifted her up and pushed forward. Barbie had no choice but to scramble down.

Then she saw Georgia and Jon. They appeared at the top of the down escalator, scrambling madly to go down as quickly as possible. "Meet you at the bottom," shouted Jon as he and Georgia passed.

Barbie almost choked in indignation. How can Jon possibly expect to meet me and my captor below? Don't they see Yannis at my back? Probably with his knife drawn? Crazy Jon.

"Where? Down? How?" she shouted, even as she tried to beat the upward push of the awkward steps.

Soon she saw Jon at the bottom with his arms held wide, waiting to receive her. Georgia stood at his shoulder, wearing a beaming grin on her face. Barbie forgot the knife at her back and the grip on her arm. Jon was safe and waiting for her.

A shout and the sound of running feet momentarily distracted Jon. He turned towards the gang of uniformed Singaporean police who raced up to them at the bottom of the escalator. Barbie stopped to take in the scene, but immediately felt her captor behind her, once more shoving her forward.

They popped off the moving steps in tandem at the bottom. "What took you so long?" demanded Yannis.

Barbie turned and saw Yannis, standing behind her, knife tucked out of sight, pretending to be glad to see the police.

"What, what is the matter? But, but, but…" Barbie sputtered. She looked at the two-faced evil man at her side. "You, you…"

Jon looked at his mother and smiled gently. "Don't worry. You are safe now."

Barbie's eyes widened in disbelief at Jon's cavalier attitude.

Jon chuckled at her bewildered face. "Oh," he said. "Didn't we tell you? He's on our side."

Chapter Thirty: Finding Matt

The four, now fast friends, had claimed places on the sofa and arm chairs at Georgia's flat. The night was almost over; a hint of pink threatened the gray in the eastern sky. Dishes of cheese and plates of crackers and chips lay strewn on the coffee table top. The smell of reheating pizza wafted from the kitchen as Jon appeared, holding one bottle of beer. He announced, "This is it, who wants to share with me?"

Yannis lifted his head from the back of the couch and mumbled, "Love it, bro!"

Georgia appeared immediately behind him, with a chilled bottle of champagne and a handful of glasses. She flopped onto the couch next to Yannis. "Okay, I guess us ladies can kill this one by ourselves."

"Don't mix your drinks," warned Jon.

"I'm so tired, I'll take anything," Barbie murmured. She held her hand out for a glass of the sparkling wine. She smiled as she watched Georgia twist off the wire top and expertly pull out the cork. She poured a generous amount into a glass and handed it to Barbie. Barbie sipped a bit, felt revived and then sat up straighter. "Wooow, what time is it anyway?"

"Who wants to know?" Jon answered. "I see the sun is about to rise, so the answer is 'very late', or 'very early', depending on your version of the night."

"Okay, skip the hour of the day, or night. I want to know what hasn't been told." Barbie sat up and looked at Yannis. "What did you tell the cops that you didn't tell me?"

Yannis looked at Barbie and slowly opened his mouth.

"I told you we could trust him, didn't I?" Georgia cut in.

"Somehow or other, when that knife appeared, I forgot about that. I forgot that Georgia said you could be trusted. I just thought it was a case of 'Oh Georgia and her bad choice in men again'. Thanks for saving me, by the way, but it would have been a lot easier if you had just told me that you were one of the good guys. And that knife and the arm pinching, was that a ploy to fool me?" Barbie said, turning to Yannis.

"Wait a minute," Georgia wailed, spilling her drink down her front. "I don't always have bad choice in men. That seems to be your forte, if I remember rightly."

"Not all the time," Barbie countered. "Don't forget the Egyptian, one of the good ones. And don't get me off the topic. Jon, when did you find out that Yannis was a good guy?"

"He was the one who tied me up," Jon laughed. "And he made the ropes and the tape a little loose. As he did it, he whispered in my ear. So, I guess I knew all along."

"And I have my own question," Georgia said. "Was I the only one who really believed in the treasure, besides the Chinese?"

"You mean the treasure that wasn't a treasure? The treasure we all looked for, ran all over Singapore trying to figure out where and what it was?" Barbie interrupted.

Yannis sighed. "A miscommunication there. I knew, but I pretended not to know just so that you would find the final piece of the puzzle. The sign of the 'jin', the gold sign. Sorry to have put you in danger. Well, not so much danger. You were never in any real danger. Not much. Really not much."

"Wait a minute," Barbie said, wrinkling her forehead. "You were supposed to be running from the cops, hiding out behind the wall in the park. Not showing up in Geylang. But at the Bras Basah Center, you seemed to know the police. You said, um…"

Yannis interrupted her. "I am the cops. Or rather, I work with the cops, undercover." His lips lifted in a half smile, half smirk. It was the kind of expression that melts hearts, makes everyone love the man.

"You're a cop?" Barbie sighed deeply, trying to take it all in.

"Well, undercover, international. I can't say anything more than that." Yannis took a deep swig of beer.

"Where's Matt?" Georgia asked. "You know where he is. You have always known. Why did you make us all jump hoops?"

"You can call him. You've had his number all this time." Yannis gave Georgia a knowing look. "You know, like Dorothy and the ruby slippers?"

"What? I did try to call. I even called the 'alternate' number. Nothing. What do you mean I've had his number all along?"

"You found the phone, didn't you?"

"Yeah, but what does that mean?" Georgia looked puzzled.

"I've got the list," Barbie volunteered. She reached for her bag and pulled out her small notebook. Here they are. 'Bru', Bruce Lee, 'Geo,' that's you. Then 'Li', which we figured out must be Mrs. Li or Mrs. Lee, the landlady, then 'Wu'."

"Mr. Wu, our calligraphy teacher," Georgia said.

"Not your nicest teacher ever," Jon put in. "Accessory to murder."

"X-L-U. What's that? Who's that?" Barbie read from her notes.

The four looked at one another. Georgia lifted her gaze to the ceiling. They all watched her.

Finally, Jon blurted out, "Xiao Lu. Little Lu. The owner of the gold shop. The chief conspirator. And murderer."

Georgia shivered at the thought. "And who else's phone number do we have?"

"YS," Barbie read out. "Yannis S (something)."

"Good enough," Yannis said.

"And then we have 'Z'," Barbie read. "And a phone number, with only seven digits."

Georgia turned to Yannis, "That's it, isn't it? Without the Singaporean first number?"

"Why don't you try?" Yannis laughed.

Georgia did as Yannis suggested, hurriedly and, Barbie thought, a bit angrily. Barbie leaned forward and listened.

After two rings, there was a 'click' and a soft, "Hello".

Georgia growled into the phone, "Where are you? I've been looking for you, everywhere. With everyone."

Barbie listened for the answer, but most of the message was garbled. She did hear, "…window." Georgia got up and moved to the large picture window that overlooked the front of the building. She pulled the drapes back. Barbie was right behind her. They both looked out.

Below them, in the quickly brightening light, they could see a solitary figure. He looked up, grinned and waved. Barbie recognized the smile of the man in the photos with Georgia. "That's him? That's Matt?"

Georgia ended the phone call without saying anything more. She watched as Matt walked into the building. Barbie stood beside her. "That's it?" Barbie marveled. "Just a phone call and he comes loping along?"

Georgia shrugged and headed for the door. She paused, staring at it for a moment or two, then opened it. As if on cue, Matt appeared at the top of the staircase. He wore a goofy grin. Georgia stepped back and held the door for him. Halfway through it, Georgia stopped him. "Where have you been?"

In response, Matt smiled, "I'm here!"

Barbie stepped forward and extended her hand, "Hi, my name is Barbie, and this is my son Jon." As Matt entered the apartment, Barbie threw Georgia a strange glance. Her boyfriend has been missing for five days, she has gone to extremes to find him, and this is how she greets him? "And of course, you know Yannis?"

Matt immediately grabbed Yannis' hand and clapped him on the back. Jon stood and received a similar greeting.

Barbie waited to be acknowledged. Finally, Matt turned to her and bowed formally. "Thank you. Thanks for being here."

Georgia had disappeared into the kitchen and reappeared with a cold can of Coke. She extended the can to Matt, "Unless of course, you want some champagne?"

"You know I promised my mother when I left that never a drop of alcohol would cross my lips," Matt replied with a smile.

"So, you say! What else have you told me that is the truth? Mostly lies, I think." Georgia looked skeptical.

Matt smiled at her again. Barbie now understood how Georgia could get involved, be intrigued, sucked into, but still question this man.

"So, are you an undercover cop too?" Georgia asked.

In answer Matt smiled again.

"Right," she answered herself. "He never lied to me," she said to the room in general. "He just never told me the truth."

Then she turned on him. "How could you do this to me? How could you involve my friends in this? You know, at first it was kind of fun. Where is Matt? Why doesn't he call? Meet Yannis in the park, what fun. Intrigue. But tonight? That wasn't a joke. Guns, blood, knives, cops, chasing some stupid treasure that was a non-treasure. What were you thinking?"

"My job, and looking for a little help from you. I didn't mean to get you in so deep," Matt answered. "Believe me, I never intended this to go so far. I just knew that you were on my side."

"Bruce Lee died," Jon said. "Whose side was he on?"

Chapter Thirty-One: Whose Side Are You On?

Barbie, Georgia and Jon stared at Matt, now standing side by side with Yannis. Barbie suddenly realized that Matt and Yannis, the undercover cops, knew a lot they weren't telling, yet this information involved innocent people. Was Bruce Lee another innocent or was he on the wrong side?

Georgia was the first to say it, "Yeah, how did it happen? Bruce Lee getting shot. Who killed him, and why did he have to die?"

"Yeah," Barbie added. "I had that gun in my face. Was that just a 'I had no intention of involving you' bit as well?"

Matt sat down heavily on the couch, his face a mask. Barbie realized that he, too, had dark circles under his eyes and the look of someone who hadn't slept much.

"Okay, okay. I'll tell you what I can. Some things I can't. State secrets, other kinds of security. But you deserve to know." Matt looked at each of them in appeal.

"Careful what you say, buddy," Yannis warned. "But I will tell you this," he said turning to the three 'innocents'. "Don't get too teary-eyed over Bruce Lee. He wasn't one of the good guys. No one, well, almost no one, deserves to die the way he did. But he wouldn't have hesitated to pull the trigger on the one who killed him."

"Who did kill him?" asked Georgia.

"He was dead when I got there," Yannis said. "So, whoever had the gun probably did it."

"When I first got there, Mr. Wu, your wonderful calligraphy teacher was wielding the gun. But soon after that, Xiao Lu grabbed it from him. So, perhaps Mr. Wu was the happy trigger finger, but it could have been Xiao Lu." Jon shook his head. "If we knew who did that, then we'd have our man."

"Either of them, I'd say, but my money is on Xiao Lu." Matt sighed. "Mr. Wu, our calligraphy teacher, dedicated to the fine arts of centuries past; he had made connections to organizations all over Asia. Hong Kong, Taiwan, Japan, Vietnam and China, all connections that he used to transport drugs. And I don't mean the fake Viagra kind, but the hard stuff."

Georgia gasped, and Barbie's eyes bulged.

"And no," Matt held his hand up. "I can say no more. I won't. I've exposed myself too much even saying this."

"So, what role did Xiao Lu play? If Mr. Wu was the contact person, what involvement did Xiao Lu have?" asked Georgia. "And why do you think he was the one who shot Bruce Lee?"

"Xiao Lu owned the antique store, the gold store. He was a greedy man," Matt said. "Or rather, he is a greedy man. That's why I fed him the story of the gold, the 'lost treasure' story. I knew that he was the linchpin in the drug business, or rather, I was informed."

"Are you telling us the truth? Or lies?" Georgia said.

"Or too much?" Yannis said cautiously. "Xiao Lu will undoubtedly go down for something, but I'm not convinced he will be convicted of the murder. There were others there, Mr. Wu, for one. And don't forget the bookstore owner."

"I was only supposed to catch the one, Xiao Lu, but through Mr. Wu. He was easy to get to know, as you well know," Matt said, turning to Georgia. "He was open to the public, gave lessons. I only meant to catch him for the smuggling. In the end, it's a judicial matter, and has nothing to do with me."

"But the story of the missing gold. You didn't make that up, I read it in the book," Barbie said. "That was real."

Matt turned to Barbie. "So, what did you read in the book? What did I tell Georgia? What was real and what was made up? Maybe I embellished the story a little, turning something that was true into a fantasy. Maybe I made up things to lure the criminals."

"But that is cheating! And the evidence against them wouldn't stick if you were luring them. I mean, in America that is enticement. Not a good way of getting a conviction." Barbie added her scant lawyerly knowledge.

"But why did you disappear, Matt?" asked Georgia. "I mean, couldn't you just hide out from Mr. Wu and the other bad guys and not make me so worried?"

"It wasn't going to work that way. I needed to be seen to be out of town or out of touch. And you went to Mr. Wu, didn't you? You went looking for me. And that gave him the idea that something was up."

"Like a shipment coming in, or the fake gold treasure," Jon added. "But why did we need to be in the dark? Couldn't you have just told Georgia to go ask Mr. Wu if he had seen you?"

"Hah! Then Georgia would have known something was really wrong. Remember, she has just now found out what kind of person I am. She is too smart, and at the same time, guileless. If I could convince her I had really disappeared, then she would convince the others too."

"But you called me on the phone, didn't you? That was you! You got me totally involved," Georgia said angrily.

"And you did wonderfully. No problems, were there? Just our gold diggers (pardon the pun) didn't get curious enough or follow you closely enough."

"But why did you need her to go to the Haw Par Villa?" Jon asked.

"Ah, I wanted you all to go, but just the once. I wanted you to be seen searching for the sign of the 'jin', which was the clue. But the stupid man didn't follow you, he missed the connection. He was supposed to find the sign of the 'jin' and then go back later. You were not supposed to go with him."

"But we didn't go with him, did we? We went with the moron bookshop owner, and your dear friend Yannis, who pretended to be on the wrong side," Georgia said, beginning to fume.

"So, we had to become lambs to the slaughter," Barbie said. "Because they screwed up!"

"You didn't have to go back to the Bras Basah Center. That was not a good move," Matt said sadly.

"Let me go back over this again. You involved me, and my friends, just to make it look good? And Yannis here, scared us half to death by pretending to be a bad guy, when he could have saved us? Much earlier?" Georgia's voice climbed another octave. Barbie knew her friend was genuinely angry this time. "Where were you all this time?"

"Not far."

"That's all you have to say, 'Not far'?" Georgia's face hardened into cement.

"Oh, I've got a few questions I want answered," Barbie said, trying to diffuse the tension. "Who messed up Matt's apartment?"

Yannis grinned at her. "I did," he said. "I tried to scare you off."

"And the little hangman's noose?" Georgia jumped in again. "Was it supposed to scare me off?" She paused. "Not funny."

"I never thought it was funny. International drug smuggling is not funny," Matt said in a tone that indicated a finality to the conversation.

"Wait a minute," Georgia persisted. "You owe me. I paid your rent, to Mrs. Lee. A $150. Otherwise, she was going to…"

A slow grin split Matt's face. "Ah, Mrs. Lee. I'll get the money back. Shame on her!"

"What?" Georgia said.

"She's one of us," Matt said simply.

Georgia rolled her eyes again.

Matt took a piece of pizza and walked away from the small group.

Barbie got up and followed him to the entrance to the kitchen. "Hmmm, I have a question for you. You work internationally, don't you?"

Matt turned to her, "Yes, I do."

"So, do you have a chance to meet other agents, other undercover cops? From other places in the world?"

"I do, sometimes. Why do you ask? Do you want to join us?" Matt grinned at her. Even though he was tired, disheveled, and looked much older than the photos Barbie had seen of him, she understood the attraction he held for Georgia.

"I was just wondering if you had ever run across an Egyptian. Tallish, about so tall," Barbie indicated a few inches above her head. "Mustache." She swiped at her upper lip. "Dark complexion, very white teeth. Sometimes goes by the name of David?"

"Very handsome? Attractive, very attractive to women? Is well-educated, clever, well-traveled?" Matt asked.

"You know him? You've met him?" Barbie gasped. "Where is he?"

"Oh, I haven't seen him, never met him!" Matt said.

"Then, how do you know..." Barbie stammered.

"Georgia told me about him," Matt said. "He must be quite a guy!"

Barbie blushed a deep red and turned around to Georgia, "You rat? How did you know so much? You weren't even in Egypt!!

Georgia approached the two of them. "That night in Cappadocia, when you saw the man fall to his death? You drank too much raki. You told me then. Ah, Barbie's secrets."

"That's why I have always heeded my mother's advice. I never drink alcohol. It can make you into a devil, and make you do dangerous, stupid things." Matt turned to Barbie, "If I ever meet him, I will say 'hello'."

Barbie hid her face by going to the couch where Jon sat. She slowly lowered herself next to him. She took his hand and squeezed it. "I'm so glad that you are safe! And I am so glad you could make it here to be with me."

"I am too, glad I'm safe, and glad to be here with you. Mom, some of the 'miss you this time' stuff was my fault as well. I mean, what a jerk I was, going off to live with dad. I just needed a little freedom, not a whole lot of chaos. I didn't really mean to hurt you, I was being selfish. But when you went abroad, just leaving me there, I felt vindictive. I never meant it all to get out of hand. But," he said with a lopsided grin, "all's well that ends well, heh?"

"It's okay. We still have each other, we still have this," she said, giving him a bump on his arm with hers. "I'd never forgive myself if something had happened, though."

"You've said that already," Jon said, yawning. "I'm falling asleep..." He leaned over onto the couch, closed his eyes and, like the youth he was, fell asleep.

Matt and Georgia were at the door. Matt was protesting that he had to go, but Georgia seemed to be trying to persuade him to stay for a while. Barbie realized that the whining and bickering she had witnessed were part of the relationship. A few minutes ago, Georgia was itching to strangle him, now they were best friends again. Barbie thought she would never understand Georgia and her relationship to men.

"I have to go, this is my job, my life," Matt protested.

"Here, just wait, I have something for you. She reached over to a small cabinet by the entrance to her room. "This is yours; don't forget it."

As she placed the small box in his hands, a huge smile crossed his face. "Oh, I thought I'd lost it, gone forever." He caressed the small box and then opened it. Barbie knew there wasn't much inside, just gold dust, but the sight lit his face. "My home is in here, you know. Now I can go anywhere; just as long as I have this." His hand enveloped the box. "Thanks," he whispered.

"Too bad this was the only real gold in the story. It's pretty, but there's not much of it," Georgia said. "I hope this is the end of the gold. Is it?"

Matt didn't answer, only looked into her eyes.

Barbie looked out the window. The sun strained to rise above the rooftops. Pale blue sky morphed into streaks of molten gold near the horizon. It had been an extraordinary day, and way too long. She felt an enormous yawn reach up from the depths of her diaphragm. She gave into it. Bed, where's my bed?

Georgia had persuaded Matt to stay, it appeared. Barbie felt a twinge of jealousy about Georgia's Singapore Fling as she watched them twine fingers on their journey to the bedroom.

Barbie turned to look at Jon as he snored while full length on the couch. Barbie headed to her guest room. At the door, she paused.

Yannis lay neatly on one side of her bed, his knees pressed together, arms folded into his armpits. He snored softly. Barbie opened her mouth to say something, but then just shrugged.